RECOVERY ROAD

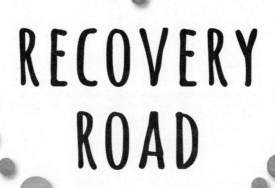

RECOVERY ROAD

BLAKE NELSON

SCHOLASTIC INC.

ISBN 978-0-545-10730-3

10 9 8 7 6 5 4 3 2 1   15 16 17 18 19

Printed in the U.S.A. 40
First printing 2015

The text was set in Alisal Regular.
Book design by Christopher Stengel

To Nicholas, Fahs, Gordon,
and Skiegs and all my
brothers at PS 51

And Something's odd — within —

That person that I was —

And this One — do not feel the same —

—EMILY DICKINSON

· part one

You can't tell what Spring Meadow is from the road. The sign, nestled beneath a large oak tree, could be for a retirement village. It could be a bed-and-breakfast. It could be a corporate office or a small women's college.

The road to the main building is confusing because you think you've entered a campus of some kind, but then you drive along a row of small houses, none of which seem to hold actual families.

At the end of the road, you're faced with a low, modern building that looks like a school or an office complex. There's still no indication of the purpose of the place. There's no medical equipment, no wheelchairs, no people with clipboards. There are no guards or attendants, no one who seems equipped to handle a crisis situation.

If you arrive on a rainy night, in wet clothes, with bits of vomit still in your hair, nobody comes running to your car to help you inside. Nobody offers to clean you up. You can clean yourself up later if you want. As with many things at Spring Meadow, it's up to you.

There's a chemical smell to the main building. It's a smell you'll get used to. If your parents brought you, they will talk to Ms. Rinaldi, who takes your patient information and fills out the insurance forms. These have to be completed before they put you in a room. And if you're sixteen, of course, there are issues of guardianship and consent.

If you're shaking slightly or having trouble focusing due to extreme levels of alcohol and/or drugs in your bloodstream, well, that's your problem. It's not like the movies. Nobody gives you a shot of sedatives to calm your nerves. Nobody lays a blanket over your shoulders. Nobody puts an arm around you and tells you everything will be fine.

You stay in the main building that first night. You lie down in a cell-like room, on a too-hard mattress with a too-flat pillow, and stare at the bare yellow wall in front of you. If you've, say, stolen a car that day and driven it into a ditch, you might still be feeling the impact in your wrists and chest, you might have cuts, scrapes, and bruises from the air bag. You might see things coming at you at high speed when you close your eyes. That's not fun. But that's nobody's problem but your own.

In a couple days you will be cleaned up, clothed, your stomach settled, your vision cleared. You will walk around the main building in your bathrobe and your slippers, with your herbal tea and your daily schedule in your pocket. Your daily schedule: drug and alcohol classes, drug and alcohol counseling, drug and alcohol group therapy sessions. There's not a lot of variety of subject matter.

But that's what it is. Spring Meadow. Rehab. That's your first twenty-eight days.

In some ways, those are the easiest.

'm trying to brush my teeth but I can't find my tooth-paste.

It's 9:30 in the morning. I'm standing in the bathroom, in my bathrobe and underwear. I've completed my twenty-eight days in the main building, and now I'm in my second week at my halfway house.

Which sucks. But it would at least be tolerable if I could brush my teeth, which I can't, because I can't find my tooth-paste.

I know I have some. I just bought it two days ago at the Rite Aid.

I open the medicine cabinet. I move stuff around. I start pulling crap out. I am sure I left it in here.

Who took my stupid toothpaste?

I shut the cabinet. The bathroom is disgusting. The floor is cold and sticks to my bare feet. The mirror is so scratched and old you can barely see yourself. I look through the shelves against the wall. They're full of cheap, abandoned beauty products. Pert shampoo. VO5 conditioner. Kroger's hand and body lotion.

I go back to my room. *Our room,* I should say, with its six bunk beds and group closet. I start digging through the shelves there, slamming things around.

Then I know who did it: Jenna. The new girl. The one who threw a hissy fit about her kitchen duties. Tough shit, Jenna. You gotta wash the dishes your first week. THAT'S HOW IT WORKS. THAT'S WHAT EVERYONE DOES.

That reminds me. Trish said something about her dental floss. She bought some and the next day it was gone. This is Jenna's doing too, no doubt.

I go into Jenna's room. I don't know which bunk is hers or which suitcase. I start tearing through the shelves and the closets.

I storm back into my own room. I am furious. I am spinning in place, looking for something to break or throw or turn over. If I had my cell phone I could call Trish right now and we could find Jenna and beat her skinny ass. But I don't have my cell phone thanks to my asshole parents who locked me in here and TOOK AWAY MY CELL PHONE LIKE I WAS SIX YEARS OLD.

I look around. I'm gonna break something BUT EVERYTHING'S BROKEN ALREADY in the stupid HALFWAY HOUSE, because it's full of CRIMINALS and DRUG ADDICTS and TEENAGE PROSTITUTES or whatever you are, JENNA, YOU STUPID BITCH.

I am really worked up now. I grab my bunk bed and shake it, smashing it against the wall until a painting falls off and breaks on the floor. Angela's secret ashtray drops through the springs of our bunk bed and scatters ashes and butts over my blankets.

I grab one of the bureau drawers and yank it out of the cabinet. Clothes fly around the room.

That's when a small white tube pops out of my bathrobe pocket, hits the floor, and bounces at my feet.

My toothpaste.

I pick it up. I look at it.

3

do not have an anger problem," I tell Cynthia, my counselor, the next day.

"Are you sure about that, Madeline?"

"No," I reluctantly admit. I'm slouched in the chair in her office. I dig at something under my nails, some green slime I got cleaning the toilets. That's what you do during your second week at the halfway house.

Cynthia stares at me like she does. "Where do you think the anger comes from?"

"From my demented brain?" I say to my thumbnail. "From my abusive childhood? Because I'm an evil bitch? How would I know?"

"You're not an evil bitch."

"I wouldn't be so sure about that," I say.

Cynthia sighs. "So how's the transition residency?"

"You mean the halfway house?" I say. "It's gross and filthy and disgusting."

"Why don't you clean it up?"

"I do clean it up. That's all I do. When I'm not working at my so-called 'job' doing laundry. I'm a teenager — I'm supposed to be working at the mall. I'm supposed to be folding sweaters at the Gap and flirting with emo boys at the Cineplex."

"Is that what you think normal teenagers do?"

"I have no idea what normal teenagers do. And I don't care either."

She watches me across her desk. "How are you getting along with the other women?"

"Let's see," I answer. "Jenna's a total criminal. Angela hates white people. Britney drinks fifteen Diet Pepsis every day and God help you if you even *touch* one of them in the refrigerator."

"I thought you said Jenna *didn't* steal your toothpaste?"

"She didn't steal *that*. It doesn't mean she's not going to steal something else. Have you seen her face? She's total trailer trash."

"What about Trish?"

"What about her?"

"You guys are the same age."

"She's eighteen. I'm sixteen. That's not the same age at all. And that's another thing. Why do we have to live with old people? I hate old people. Why can't we have a house of just young people?"

"Would that make a difference?" asks Cynthia patiently. "Would you like the people better?"

No, I admit silently to myself.

"So what's wrong with Trish?" asks Cynthia.

"Nothing's wrong with her. I just don't need any friends right now. I haven't had alcohol or drugs for thirty-eight days. Isn't that the point of all this? What else do you want from me?"

"Have you thought about how they feel? Have you considered it might be hard for Angela to be here? Or Trish? Could you maybe help them in some way?"

"Why should I help them? Why don't they help me? I mean, you lock us inside this place and then you want us to do your work for you. It's ridiculous."

"I'm just suggesting the situation might be easier if you made some friends."

"I don't want any friends! I have my own problems to worry about."

Cynthia watches me from across her desk. "You need other people, Madeline. There's a great freedom in knowing that. And accepting that. And letting people in. Letting them help you."

"Yeah, whatever," I say. "I can only do what I can do, okay?"

"If you say so."

4

fter dinner, I retreat to my bunk bed with a crossword puzzle. Trish comes into my room and stands in the doorway. If I had to describe Trish, I would say: "high school parking lot." She smokes. She wears too much makeup. She probably gives great hand jobs.

"Hey," she says.

"Hey," I say back, without enthusiasm.

"Whatcha doing?"

"Nothing."

"You wanna go to movie night?"

"Not really," I say.

"C'mon, it might be fun. You get to ride in the van."

"I've ridden in vans before."

She leans against the doorway. "There might be boys."

"I thought the boys were off-limits."

"So they say."

I frown and scratch out one of my crossword answers. "I don't want to get dressed."

"Oh God," says Trish. "Don't you want to go somewhere? Aren't you sick of sitting around here?"

I am. Massively. And it's November and all it does is rain. I've barely been outside for a week.

Trish stands at the door. I remain on my bed. She awaits my decision.

I throw my crossword puzzle on the bed.

"Good," says Trish. "I'll meet you out front."

Fifteen minutes later, we're standing on the porch. The Spring Meadow van arrives at 6:25. We climb in, Trish and me and another woman from our house.

The van continues down Recovery Road, picking up other people from the other halfway houses. There's an old gay guy in a blue blazer. There's a tattooed, middle-aged rocker dude. There's a creepy boy with big ears and a rodent face. Last but not least are two fifty-year-old women in hideous tracksuits.

The driver takes us into the town, Carlton, Oregon, which is basically one street. He pulls up in front of an old movie theater. It's called The Carlton — surprise, surprise. We pile out of the van like a bunch of retarded people.

We stand there. It's very embarrassing. We are just about the worst-looking group of human beings imaginable. If I saw us walking down the sidewalk, I wouldn't just cross the street, I'd run home and take a shower.

Trish bums a cigarette from one of the tracksuit ladies. I stand with her while she smokes. At least she and I are young. If you cleaned us up and gave us decent clothes, we might actually look presentable.

We wait. Nobody knows what movie we're seeing. Nobody knows when it starts. Nobody has a watch. Nobody goes to see.

Vern, the gay guy, finally gets the great idea to buy tickets and go inside. The rest of us follow along.

The Carlton is a dump. The lobby smells like moldy carpet. The wallpaper is peeling. It's cold, drafty, damp. Popcorn is only a buck, though. So that's good.

Trish and I get popcorns and Cokes. We stand together and stay close to Vern, so that Middle-Aged Rocker Dude can't hit on us.

In the theater, we sit in a line. Me on the far end. Then Trish. Then Vern. Then everyone else. The previews play. I zip up my coat, pull down my hat, take a long breath.

Movie night.

The film starts. It involves guns and drugs and a suitcase of money. *God, I'd love a shot of Jack Daniel's,* I think. Or a beer. Or anything.

The movie continues. I have no idea what's happening. I'm totally bored and I'm getting the squirmies. The squirmies is when your body says to your brain: WHERE IS OUR DAILY DOSE OF DRUGS AND ALCOHOL? WE WANT IT. GIVE IT TO US NOW!

I shift around in my seat. I feel like wires are being tightened inside my chest and shoulders. Or like a billion tiny insects have invaded my nervous system. I lose all focus on the movie and I clench my teeth and my fists and I feel like my whole body is being turned inside out.

Then I blank out. My brain shuts off. I forget where I am and what I'm doing. And then five minutes later, I'm okay, everything's fine, I'm totally cool. I eat some of Trish's popcorn.

That's how it goes with the squirmies.

The movie, meanwhile, continues to suck. There's an especially idiotic part where the ex-cop sees a picture of his children and remembers how much he loves them. Violins actually play.

"Who gives a shit?" Trish says out loud to the screen.

"*Shhhhh,*" says someone behind us.

It gets worse. There's a love scene that is so stupid I almost barf. Trish starts giggling. This makes me start giggling. We can't help it. People get mad. Then Trish starts laughing so hard she can't stop and she blows Coke-snot out her nose.

"Would you please be quiet?" says a man in front of us.

"Would you please eat me?" says Trish.

We finally calm down, but then during the final ten minutes, when there's car chases and explosions, we get a little carried away.

"Kill that asshole!" screams Trish when the good guy holds one of the bad guys at gunpoint.

"Shoot him in the face!" I yell.

The other moviegoers are not happy with us. We don't care. Life is ridiculous. It's not our fault.

5

Trish almost killed her best friend in a drunk-driving accident. The friend is still in the hospital. She's gonna be paralyzed, it sounds like. One of her vertebrae did something to her spinal cord.

Trish doesn't talk about it, but every couple days she calls the girls' parents, or the girl, and then for the rest of the day she barely speaks. That's how she is on Friday, so I suggest we walk up to the main building that night. That's what we do when we get depressed or have a bad day — we retreat to the main building. It's like crawling back into the womb.

Trish and I sit in the lounge and play cards. Trish steals some of the good coffee from the staff kitchen and we play gin rummy. It's a nice lounge, a lot nicer than the halfway house. The furniture isn't all stained and broken.

Trish deals us a hand. "You gonna drink when you get outta here?" she asks me, breaking her silence.

"I don't know. Are you?"

She discards. "If I do, I'm sure as hell not driving anywhere."

I draw a card from the deck. "Yeah, but how are you going to not drive? You gotta go places."

Trish shrugs. "Maybe my parents can get me a driver."

"Yeah, like a butler."

"Maybe he'll be hot. Maybe he'll be like Juan in security."

Juan in security has been Trish's crush since she got here. She also likes Dustin in the kitchen. And Sam in maintenance. You can't do much about crushes at Spring Meadow, though. There's a no-dating policy. Strictly enforced.

I drink from Trish's stolen coffee. *God, I'd love a shot of Jack Daniel's*, I think. Or a hit off a joint. Or anything.

"How do you even hang out with boys if you're not drinking?" Trish asks, taking her turn.

"I have no idea."

"It seems impossible."

I draw a card and throw it in the pile.

"I think about parties I've been to," says Trish. "And I imagine myself telling people, 'Oh, no, thank you. No beer for me.' What a joke. I could never do that."

"Maybe you have to hide out."

"I'm not going to *hide out* the rest of my life." Trish draws a card, throws it on the pile.

"Maybe there are other ways to hook up," I say.

"Cynthia says I'll still meet people," says Trish. "But what cool person our age can't drink a stupid beer?"

We abandon our game and go outside so Trish can smoke. We sit on the bench. I curl my fists up in the sleeves of my old coat.

"You got a boyfriend at home?" Trish asks me.

"I've never had a boyfriend," I answer.

"Why not?"

"I dunno. Must be my sparkling personality."

"I was trying to remember if I'd ever had sex with someone when I wasn't drunk," says Trish. "I don't think I have."

"I know I haven't."

"I wonder what it feels like," says Trish.

"Probably pretty good," I say. "The way people go on about it."

"I can't imagine doing anything straight," says Trish, her face illuminated for a moment by the burn of her cigarette. "I'll probably just kill myself. I tried that once."

"Yeah, how did that go?"

"I fucked it up. Like everything else."

"I'll probably start beating the crap out of people."

"Really?" says Trish. "You beat people up?"

"Sometimes," I say. "When I'm drunk. I'm sorta famous for it."

"Really?" says Trish. "You, like, *punch* them? With your fist?"

"Yup."

"That's awesome. That's so strong."

"It's a great way to meet police officers."

Trish thinks for a moment. "I would love to beat people up. How did you learn to do that?"

"I got really, really drunk and then it just came to me."

6

Most nights in bed, I lie awake and squirm and stare at the bottom of Angela's bunk. I think: *God, I would love a shot of Jack Daniel's. Or a vodka cranberry. Or a Vicodin. Or a bong hit.*

Other nights I'm more calm. I lie blinking in the darkness and wonder what will happen to me. Will I finish high school? Will I get a job? Will I ever get married? Have I already ruined any chance at having a normal life?

Then one night I'm half asleep and I feel my bunk move. It's Trish.

"Can I get in with you?" she whispers in the dark.

I'm not a big sleeping-with-other-people person. Especially girls. I'm sort of not into it at all. But Trish is crying. She must have talked to the girl she almost killed. There are tears running down her face.

"Okay," I say.

She gets in and I scoot over. We lie there. It's kinda weird. She can tell I don't want to cuddle or anything, so she scoots over and turns her back to me, faces away. I kind of lie on my side too, like spooning but not really touching.

We lie like that and you can tell she's trying not to cry, but she can't help it. The bed shakes as she sobs.

"Are you okay?" I finally whisper to her.

She nods, but doesn't answer. I stare at the back of her head. She's had it much worse than me. She paralyzed her best friend.

I rub her back a little and she finally falls asleep. I fall asleep too.

Then we both wake up the next morning, when Angela accidentally kicks Trish in the head.

S o tell me more about this nickname," says Cynthia in her office.

"What's there to tell?" I say. "They called me Mad Dog. Mad Dog Maddie."

"And why did they call you that?"

"Why do you think?"

"Because you were aggressive and hostile toward other people?" she asks.

"That would be why. Yes."

"Why were you like that?"

"Did you ever go to high school?"

"Yes."

"And did you notice most of the people are assholes?"

"I thought most of the people were just people."

"Well, at my high school, they're mostly assholes."

Cynthia nods. "What about the girls? Did you have any female friends?"

"Did you not hear what I just said? The people there were *assholes*."

She writes something in her notebook. I hate it when she does that.

"Did you ever fight with boys?" she asks.

"Sometimes."

"What did it feel like, hitting people, trying to hurt them?"

"Honestly?"

"Of course."

"It was fun," I say.

"Why was it fun?"

"It just was. It was exciting. It was a rush."

"So it was almost like another drug, added to the ones you were already on?"

I shrug. "I guess."

"So you weren't actually angry at these people?"

"Of course I was angry at them."

"But it wasn't really anything they did. It was more because you needed that adrenaline rush."

"Trust me. They usually did something."

She tosses her notebook on her desk. "You know there's a saying: 'If you meet three assholes in a day, you're the asshole.' Do you think that could be true?"

"That *I'm* the asshole? No! Are you kidding me?"

She stares at me.

"No way," I say. "I am *never* the asshole."

8

The next movie night, Trish and I get dressed up. We don't have much to work with but we buy some cheap makeup at the local Rite Aid and slut ourselves up as best we can.

When the van comes, it's just Vern and this woman we don't know. But Vern is in a good mood and he tells us dirty jokes all the way to Carlton. We laugh and goof around and try to gross each other out. The other woman is mostly horrified by the three of us. She's like a suburban housewife who's addicted to Ambien.

There's only about ten other people at the theater. Vern and Trish and I make fun of the movie. And talk. And gossip about Juan in security. The other people don't appreciate this. At one point someone threatens to call the manager.

"Just try it," says Trish. "My friend Maddie here will kick your ass!"

"No, I won't," I say, shrinking into my seat.

"Yes, you will. And I'll help."

• • •

Afterward, back at the halfway house, Trish and I keep everyone up late watching *America's Next Top Model* and playing gin rummy and drinking so much Diet Coke our eyes get fuzzy. Everyone tells stories about weird stuff that has happened to them with boys.

Angela tells about her cousin who started pimping her out to his friends when she was twelve.

Trish tells about losing her virginity in eighth grade when she was so drunk she couldn't stand up. "That made it easier for the Hartley brothers," she says. "I couldn't get away." This happened in her parents' pool house, while her parents were having a party. Trish's family is sort of crazy, it sounds like. You didn't even have to leave the house to get into serious trouble.

My situation was the opposite. I was so bored at home I couldn't stand it. I was always getting caught crawling out my window. Or trying to steal my mom's Volvo. Or trying to hitchhike someplace.

Everyone is horrified when I tell them about the hitchhiking. They act like *that's* the scariest thing they've ever heard of.

That night when I go to bed, I'm totally wired on Diet Coke. It's a terrible high, all chemicals and caffeine and my skin is crawling and I can barely stand it. At one point I get the squirmies so bad I kick off my covers and kick the wall about twenty times and then lie there breathing and cursing to myself.

Nobody says anything, though. Not even Angela, who's right above me.

People freaking out at night isn't that unusual at Spring Meadow. You kinda have to live and let live.

Then one day Trish starts gathering her stuff. She's finished her eight weeks in the halfway house. She's going home.

For some reason, I have refused to think of her as a real friend. But the minute I realize she's leaving, I get so panicked I almost throw up.

I sit on her bunk and watch her fold clothes and put them in her suitcase. She's worried about her cigarettes because she told her parents she quit, but she didn't. She tries hiding them in various places in her suitcase. She wonders if she should maybe try to quit now. She goes outside to smoke while she thinks about it.

I don't say very much. When Trish goes, the only young person in the house will be Jenna, and I'm not going to be friends with her. She's horrible. She's like a wild animal.

Trish gives me the makeup we bought at Rite Aid, and the barrettes and the lip gloss. She wants to give me stuff, like you do when you say good-bye to someone. I want to give her something too. But we don't have anything, just our crappy clothes, sweatpants, and the junk they let you have in here: candy bars, gum, trashy novels.

She gives me a deck of cards she forgot she had and never opened. I give her a plastic key chain that has no real significance.

"I'm really going to try to stay sober this time," she says to me quietly. "I never really tried before. I'm going to do yoga and meditate and go to AA and all that."

I nod hopefully.

I help her carry her stuff onto the porch. Then we sit and wait for her mom. I look at the arm of the chair and think of all the people who have sat here, waiting to be picked up, waiting to start a new life. Not many actually get a new life. Most people go right back to their old life. That's what Cynthia always says. The statistics are not pretty.

A black Cadillac Escalade appears. Trish's mom gets out. And her little sister. Her mom is an older version of Trish, tons of makeup, cheesy highlights, probable boob job. The little sister is dancing around in the reflection of the car windows, singing into a hairbrush. For a moment my heart sinks for Trish. This is the genius family who let her get raped in her own pool house.

Her mom picks her way across the muddy yard, trying to protect her designer shoes. But when she gets to us, she hugs Trish and I can see the strain in her face. And the worry. And the love.

It kinda kills me. It does. It breaks my heart.

The freaky sister hugs her too, and then Trish introduces me. I step forward and shake hands and the mom says, "Trish has told us all about you. She says you've been a great friend to her."

"I didn't really do anything," I mumble.

"Thank you," her mother says again, gripping my hand. "Thank you so much."

Trish and I drag her stuff to the car. The little sister is still bopping around, sticking her ass out.

Trish gets in the passenger seat. Her mom starts the car. I stand there while Trish lowers her window. "Will you call me?" she says.

I nod that I will.

The Cadillac pulls away. I stand in the street watching them go. I feel like I'm having my heart ripped out.

It's so weird being straight. You have no defenses. Shit happens and you have to feel it. You have no choice.

Without Trish, the whole house situation changes. It's just me and a bunch of old hags basically. I stay in my room as much as I can. I start reading a ragged copy of Stephen King's *The Stand*. I hide in the bathroom, picking at my toenails and reading for hours.

Later in the week, they shuffle the bunks around and we get two new people in our room. One is Margarita, a Nicaraguan woman who shot her husband in the stomach when she was drunk. The other is an ice-cold rich lady who only wears sweat clothes but spends two hours every morning putting on her makeup and fixing her hair.

God, I miss Trish.

On Monday I meet with my counselor, Cynthia, and she tells me I have to be more open to others and not judge people so fast. She says: "Your disease wants you isolated. Your disease wants you alone."

That's how they talk in rehab. Being a cranky bitch is "a disease."

Then my dad calls.

My dad is sort of a big deal. He used to be an engineer at NASA and then he ran a solar energy business and now he's a private consultant, and so he travels constantly, raising capital and talking to rich and powerful people around the world. I think he cheats on my mom on these trips, but whatever, it's for the good of the family, making truckloads of money and all.

So we talk. He's obviously really busy and doesn't have time and doesn't know what to say. But he does his best. It's better than talking to my mom at least, who always tries to tell me what to do. This has never worked, since I'm about ten times smarter than her and always do what I want anyway. But that's our family dynamic. Mom is clueless and pissed off, while my dad and I both see what totally outrageous bullshit we can get away with.

Later, back in my room, I have an argument with ice queen Sweatpants Lady, because one of my dirty socks touched her floor area.

As we "discuss" this matter, I stare at her and consider

punching her face in. I'm actually about to do it . . . but then it turns out I'm sort of a wuss when I'm not drunk.

Later still, we all learn something about Margarita, the woman who shot her husband in the stomach: She snores. It's so loud, the window shakes. It's like a wounded buffalo groaning all night, about three inches from your ear. And when she's not doing that, she's chattering in her sleep. In Spanish.

This place is a loony bin.

12

ern leaves. I find this out on the next movie night. I'm getting in the van, and I see that nobody's inside.

"Where's Vern?" I ask the driver, since Vern always goes to movie night, no matter what.

"He shipped out. Went back to Estacada."

"He's gone?"

"He'll be back," says the driver. "Vern always comes back."

I get in, pull the side door closed, and sit down. I'm stunned. No Vern? No Trish? How am I supposed to survive here?

I stare out the window. It's raining and cold and I'm wearing my own gross sweatpants tonight, which are dirty and not warm enough.

"Looks like nobody's going to the movies tonight," says the driver when we pull over at the next house.

I stare out the rain-blurred window. There's nobody there.

We continue along Recovery Road. We come to the last house. There's no one there either. But wait, there's one person.

A guy, it looks like. He's standing on the porch. He's wearing a green army coat over a hoodie.

The driver pulls the van over and the guy isn't sure what he's supposed to do. He finally hops off the porch and comes toward us. He squints in the rain.

"Is this the movie thing?" he asks the driver.

"It sure is. Hop in."

He opens the sliding door. That's when he sees that there's no one inside except me.

"Oh," he says as he looks around the empty van.

He gets in and shuts the door. He sits at the end of my seat. He's tall and skinny and has dyed blond hair. He looks like a rock star. Maybe he was rich and famous and blew it all on drugs and hookers. They get those at Spring Meadow sometimes.

"Are there more people?" he asks.

"Not tonight," says the driver.

I say nothing. I look out the window, away from him.

But then I remember I'm supposed to be nice to people — according to Cynthia — and make friends, and not judge. So I turn and try to smile at him. That's when I see how young he is. He's my age. He's just a kid.

The van drives. He doesn't say anything. He seems vaguely in shock. I know the feeling.

We drive for a while. Finally, he asks the driver what movie we're going to see.

"Beats me. I just drive."

He looks at me.

I shrug. "I just go."

"Huh," he says, staring forward in the dark.

• • •

31

It takes about fifteen minutes to get to Carlton. The driver is listening to sports talk radio. We all listen to it.

When we reach the theater, the two of us get out. Him first, then me. I shut the door. The driver waves to me and pulls away.

Then we're alone together. On the sidewalk. I avoid looking at him.

"I'm Stewart," he says.

"I'm Maddie," I reply.

"So now what do we do?" he asks me.

"We should probably go in."

We buy our tickets. We go in. The two of us stand nervously in the lobby. We look like we're on a date, which makes it even weirder than it already is.

"The popcorn's only a buck," I tell him.

"Yeah?"

"We usually get some."

"Then let's get some."

We go to the concession counter. A local boy, about fourteen, gets us our popcorn. He stares up at tall, imposing Stewart with a mixture of awe and fear.

Inside the actual theater there's more awkwardness. Should we sit next to each other or one seat apart? I end up making this decision and sit one seat apart. But then some other people come and we are forced to sit together.

We don't speak. In the dim light of the previews, I sneak looks at him. He has dark, watery eyes, pale white skin. His face is chiseled, with high, wide cheekbones. He's totally cute, is the truth of it.

I, on the other hand, am wearing bag-lady sweatpants and a down coat with food stains on it. I'm also bloated and I smell and my hair is dirty.

But whatever.

I sneak more looks. He's got a tattoo on the inside of his left wrist and a small silver ring on his right pinkie. It looks like a girl's ring. I wonder whose it is.

During the movie he fidgets. He just got out of the main building, which means he's still in partial squirmies mode. He bites his nails, strokes his hair, shifts around in his seat.

When the lights come on, we both have our feet draped over the seats in front of us. For some reason neither of us gets up right away. The other people file out. They stare at us as they leave, like: *Who are these lowlifes in the back?*

Stewart's definitely got the bad-ass thing going on. He doesn't look like someone you'd want to meet in a dark alley.

Finally, he stands up. I stand up. I follow him through the lobby and out of the theater.

We stand on the cold street. More painful silence.

"So what happens now?" Stewart asks.

"We usually go to the donut place. And then the van comes."

"Okay," he says.

At the donut place, we stand in line behind some local high school kids. They're laughing, teasing each other, goofing around. They don't notice us at first but then one of the girls turns and sees Stewart standing over her and she shuts right up.

We order coffees and donuts. Stewart pulls some crap out of his pocket and finds a couple wadded-up dollar bills to pay. He goes to a booth by the window and sits. I follow and sit across from him.

I'm having a sugar craving so I put six sugar packets in my coffee. Stewart watches me do this but says nothing.

I drink some of it, sipping it carefully because it's hot. It's too hot. I put it down and take a big bite of my glazed twister donut.

Stewart takes a bite of his jelly donut.

"I get on these sugar things sometimes," I say as I put two more sugars into my coffee.

"That's a lot of sugar," he says.

"I can't sleep anyway. So what's the difference?"

"Yeah, sleeping's tough."

He looks out the window. The high school kids walk across the parking lot. They're happy American teenagers. They unlock their car from ten feet away. They laugh. One jumps on the back of another.

I glance up at Stewart's face. He's so handsome it's kinda hard to deal with. So I look at his hands. They're knobby and beat up. One of the knuckles has a big scar across it.

"How old are you?" I ask him.

"Nineteen," he says. "You?"

"Seventeen," I say. But then I decide not to lie. "I mean, almost. I'll be seventeen in a couple weeks."

He drinks his coffee.

"Yeah," I say. "I had this friend Trish. She was eighteen. We were the only younger people in our house, but then this other girl Jenna came. She's weird, though."

He looks across the table at my coffee cup. "Sixteen. That's pretty young."

"Yeah," I say. "I got into stuff pretty early."

"Yeah. Me too."

"It just sorta . . . rolled over me."

"Yeah," he says. "I know."

The van ride back is quick. Too quick. I want to talk more. Not because Stewart is cute. I kind of wish he wasn't so cute. It's just that he's easy to talk to. Or not even. He's easy to sit with. I just like him, I guess.

But he's lost in his own thoughts as we drive back. And I can't think of anything to say. When we get back to his house, he gets out and I find myself saying, "See ya," and waving my hand in this stupid way. He looks at me funny and slams the door shut.

The van continues up the street.

And then something really weird happens: Tears come into my eyes. For no apparent reason I actually cry for a second.

"How was the flick?" asks the driver.

I wipe the tears away. "It was okay," I say in the dark.

"What was it about?" he asks.

"I have no idea."

13

The next day, my dad comes to see me. He shows up in his new BMW and we drive into Carlton.

We go to the one nice restaurant in town. We sit at the table with our napkins in our laps. My dad is tanned, handsome, wearing a nice suit. The local people gawk at him. He doesn't mind. He likes being a star. Of course he wants to hear about me, but he can't resist telling me about a new project he's doing and how he's getting the money from these Japanese guys who invented robotic pets.

Then he does the fatherly thing and puts on a concerned expression and asks me how my life is going.

The thing about my dad is, he was a big partier himself. He still is. And so, in his mind, what's happened to me is that I can't "handle" stuff. He thinks my problem is a lack of control. Which is true. In a way.

We eat our lunch. He makes a big deal about how good his chicken is. He flirts with the waitress and leaves her a big tip.

Back at the halfway house, we park in the street. He wants to come in and see it, but I tell him he doesn't really want to, it's depressing, so he doesn't.

"Your mom and I talked to your principal at Evergreen," he tells me. "It sounds like you can re-enroll after Christmas. There are some summer school options too. This is all dependent on how things go, of course. And what Dr. Bernstein says."

I don't answer. I don't want to go back to my old high school. "Maybe I could get a GED," I say.

"Why would you do that?" my father says. "There's no reason to miss out on the rest of high school."

"What do I need high school for?"

"Because," he says. "It's part of life. You still have your whole senior year to go."

"But what am I going to do there? Who am I going to hang out with?"

"You'll make new friends. High school isn't just about hanging out."

"What's it about, then?"

"It's about studying. And preparing for college."

That's going to be another sore spot with my parents. They're still going to want me to go to college.

"I don't think a GED is what you want," he says. "If you really think about it."

"I know I don't want to go back to Evergreen," I say, unfastening my seat belt. "Do you have any idea how many people there hate my guts?"

"Probably fewer than you think," says my dad. "Will you just think about it? We don't have to decide anything right now."

Predictably, the call from my mother comes the same night. I have to take it on the house phone, in front of everyone. We have one of our classic conversations:

"Your father said you had a nice lunch."

"That's right," I say, waiting for the argument to start.

"He said it was a very constructive conversation."

"Yes, it was," I say, waiting for the argument to start.

"The one thing that sounded strange to me, he said you wanted to get a GED."

"That's right, that's what I said."

"But, Madeline, why would you do that?"

"Because, Mom. That's what people do in these situations."

"But you used to like school."

"I kinda burned that bridge, Mom. So now I have to do the logical thing, which is get a GED."

"But why?"

I turn to the wall. "So I don't have to go back there in total humiliation!"

"Nobody is going to humiliate you. People forgive people."

"Forgiveness is not the issue, Mom."

"What would you do otherwise? Even if you got a GED where would you go? You're sixteen. You can't get a full-time job."

"Mom, I'll be seventeen in three weeks. A lot of people get jobs when they're seventeen. I'll go to community college."

"It just makes no sense to me. Your father is very hopeful about the situation. He is doing everything he can."

"Everything he can? Are you serious? Do you know where I am right now, Mom? Do you know where I sleep?"

"I understand that, dear —"

"I sleep in bunk beds, Mom. With people who shot people!"

"Honey, I understand that. But you need to understand this has been a burden on us as well. Your father has been worried sick. Do you know how much Dr. Bernstein charges? And it's not all covered by insurance, you know."

"All right, Mom. Okay. I'm the evil daughter and you guys are the victims."

"I'm not saying that. All I'm saying is why can't you at least consider his advice? A lot of people consider your father a very intelligent man."

"Okay, Mom, I gotta go."

"We've spent a lot of time on this. I've had conversations with Dr. Bernstein almost every day."

"All right, all right, I'll think about it," I say. I am now in a hurry because Margarita just turned on *America's Next Top Model*, which is my new favorite show.

"That's all we ask."

"Okay, gotta go." I hang up and go straight to the TV.

14

Two days later, I'm reading *Us Weekly* at my laundry room job and I happen to glance outside and see the maintenance crew doing something to the lawn. One of them is Stewart. He's wearing coveralls. His dyed blond hair sticks out from beneath a baseball cap.

I go to the window and watch the group of them. They talk, they poke at the ground with shovels. Not a lot of work gets done. Stewart stands apart, the baby of the group.

I sit on the windowsill. I watch Stewart. I watch him lean against the truck. I watch him drink coffee. I watch him take a shovel out of the truck, lean on it, and then put it back.

Eventually, the crew gets back in its truck and drives away. I go back to my chair and pick up my magazine. I try to read but I can't concentrate. Not now. I go back to the window and stare out at the empty lawn.

I think through my night with Stewart at The Carlton theater. What he said. What I said. The way he looked standing on the sidewalk. The squareness of his shoulders, the silence in his face . . .

Then I tear myself away and go back to my chair. I don't know what I'm daydreaming about. I've been with tons of guys. It never works out.

I snatch up my *Us Weekly*. It's ridiculous to even think about.

15

Movie night comes around again. It's all I've been
thinking about. I sneak down to Rite Aid the day
before, where I wander the aisles looking for something to make me halfway attractive to a boy.

It won't be easy. I'm pale, blotchy. I've gained eight pounds
of "recovery fat." I've got deep bags under my eyes. I try different shades of lip gloss. I experiment with eye shadow. I sneak
a pinch of Preparation H and rub it under my eyes.

Back at the house, I go through my stuff. I have one cute
skirt at the bottom of my suitcase. I put it on. I find my favorite blue socks and put those on. I put on my one clean shirt and
brush out my hair.

Margarita watches all this from her bunk. "Big night for
you, no?" she asks.

"It's movie night."

"You dress up? Just for movie?"

There's no point lying about it. "There was a boy there last
time," I say.

"Ahhhh. Movie night!"

I check my hair in the mirror. "You wanna go?"

"No, no. No boys for me. I shoot my husband."

"It might be good practice. You know, for not shooting people."

"No. You go. Have good time."

I wait on the porch. When the van comes, I run to it. There are people already inside: two older women and a skinny guy with taped-together glasses.

We go to the next stop, two more people get in. It's going to be crowded tonight. I don't know if that's good or bad. At the final stop I crane my neck to see if Stewart is on the porch. . . .

He is.

I instantly sit back in my seat, sink down into it, curl my hands in my coat pockets. What on earth am I doing? What do I think is going to happen?

He gets in. An older guy gets in with him. They're talking.

I am in the farthest-back seat with one of the women. Stewart and his friend squeeze onto the first bench seat. They're deep in conversation. I sit forward slightly and try to listen. They're talking about drugs.

I did drugs too, I want to shout. *I did tons of drugs. I did painkillers and smoked hash and snorted coke. I got arrested. I stole a car. I slept with a drug dealer and got thrown out of my own house. I . . . I . . . I . . .*

I sit back and close my eyes. I bow my head. I pray to God to please not let me make a complete ass of myself tonight.

"Hey, Maddie," Stewart says when he sees me getting out of the van.

"Hey," I say casually.

His older guy friend is heading inside, but Stewart hangs back. He waits for me. "I didn't see you sitting back there."

"Oh yeah," I joke. "I'm a back-of-the-van sorta girl."

He smiles at this. It warms me all over.

We walk along behind the other people. We buy our tickets. Stewart doesn't say anything but he seems to want to stay near me.

It makes sense. We're the only ones under thirty in the entire group.

"You want popcorn?" I ask Stewart in the lobby.

"Sure," he says, and he comes with me. The same pimply local boy scoops us out two bags of popcorn. He smiles up at Stewart respectfully.

We go into the theater and sit with the other people. We're on the end. We sit right next to each other.

The previews start. I find myself laughing at stuff that's not even funny. Mostly because I'm so nervous.

The movie plays. It's a supernatural horror thriller. I hadn't realized this. Scary movies freak me out.

I get through it by closing my eyes and humming to myself during the worst parts. Stewart doesn't seem to notice. At least, he doesn't say anything.

When the lights come up, we all shuffle out. The group of us cross the street to the donut place. I'm trying to stick near Stewart but then his guy friend comes over and grabs him away. I get stuck walking with two women I don't know.

Which pisses me off.

Inside the donut place, our group takes up two tables. I get stuck in the coffee line, and end up sitting far away from Stewart. There's nothing I can do. I watch him from afar. He sits there: shy, silent, adorable. Everyone loves him. The older women especially. They want to hold him to their bosoms. It kills me to see this.

The men dominate the conversation. They tell their usual war stories: The time they got arrested. The time they crashed their car.

Whatever.

I try not to stare at Stewart. How can I not? He is beautiful and sad and perfect in some fascinating way. If only it was the two of us. If only we could talk.

The clock is against me. Only nine more minutes until the van comes. I stare into my coffee. He's forgotten I'm here, so it doesn't make any difference. I don't know what I was thinking.

But then at 9:30, when we all gather outside, he comes over to me.

"Hey," he says.

"Hey," I say back.

I try to think of something else to say. "I saw you with the maintenance crew," I manage.

"You did?"

"You were out in the lawn."

"Oh yeah. Fixing the sprinklers."

"What happened to the sprinklers?"

"They break sometimes in the winter."

"Oh."

The van comes. Everyone gets in. I sit in the back and slouch down like I do. Other people get in. Stewart gets in. He comes back and sits beside me.

"I guess I'm a back-of-the-van person too," he says, smiling.

We drive. We're sitting pretty far apart. But I look over at him and he kind of looks at me and then he laughs.

"What?" I say.

"I don't know. It's just funny."

"What's funny?"

"That we meet like this," he says.

"What? In a van?"

"No, just . . . the whole thing."

We're talking quietly, so that the other people won't hear. They're all caught up in their own conversations anyway.

"I don't see what's so funny about it," I say.

"Maybe it's not funny."

"I'm glad you're sitting here," I tell him, my heart pounding as I say it.

"Yeah?"

"I wish we coulda talked more tonight," I say.

He stares straight ahead. "Yeah," he says. "Me too."

I look away. My heart is thudding in my chest. I watch out the window as a farmhouse drifts by.

I turn back to him. I summon every ounce of courage I possess. "Maybe we should meet up somewhere," I say quietly.

He looks at me, surprised. "I thought boys weren't supposed to . . . you know . . . fraternize with girls."

"So we won't. We'll just hang out."

He looks at me in the dark. "Where would we do that?"

"How about the Rite Aid, tomorrow at eight."

He thinks about the Rite Aid. He thinks about it a long time.

"Or not," I finally say. "If you don't want to."

"No," he says. "That might be okay."

17

The next day, I am very businesslike as I go about my routine. I get up, get dressed, walk through the rain to my job at the laundry room. I wash sheets for three hours and then go to my group therapy, where I make up some crap about my parents so I can space out and think about meeting Stewart.

After that, I go home and eat dinner and watch *Access Hollywood* with my housemates. At 7:30, I go to my room and change my clothes. Margarita is reading on her bunk. I look at myself in the mirror. I glance down at Margarita, who smiles at me innocently.

Is it wrong to meet Stewart? I wonder. I hadn't really thought about that.

When I'm ready, I find an old umbrella in the main closet. It's broken of course, but it'll work. I go outside and open it, and then stand for a moment on the porch. A strange feeling comes over me then, as I stare into the dark street. It's not fear exactly. It's more like a sense of the mystery of the world.

But whatever. I've got a cute boy to meet. I hop down the porch steps and set out through the rainy night.

The Rite Aid is bright and clean inside. I shake the water from my umbrella. I walk around in my wet Converse. I cruise around once really fast, but I'm early, and I see that Stewart's not here yet. I try to relax then. I read some greeting cards.

Eight o'clock comes. I walk through the aisles again, looking at the candy and the holiday stuff. A Christmas song is playing: *Chestnuts roasting on an open fire . . .*

Where is he? I wonder. But I'm not mad. Not like I used to get.

Now I'm just numb.

He doesn't come. It gets to be 8:20. 8:30. 8:40. I am sitting on the floor by the magazines when the manager finds me and tells me they close at 9:00. He is remarkably nice, considering I've been sitting on his floor for an hour, ruining his magazines.

At 8:50, I pick out some gum to buy. I don't know where Stewart is. I tell myself it's okay. He probably freaked out. Who wouldn't, having some sixteen-year-old throwing herself at you? He probably thinks I'm out of my mind.

I finally walk up to the counter, and there, to my surprise, is Stewart, red-faced and wet.

"Hey," he says, out of breath. "Sorry I'm late."

"It's okay," I say.

I buy my gum. Stewart waits for me. He's wearing the same skinny jeans, the hoodie, the military coat.

"I couldn't get away," he says. "That guy from the movie cornered me."

"Did he not want you to come?"

"I didn't tell him."

I give him a piece of gum. "People here are kind of crazy," I say. "Have you noticed that?"

"Yeah," he says.

Outside, we chew our gum. We stand by the door of the Rite Aid and stare into the dripping darkness. We look at each other and kind of just . . . look at each other.

18

We decide to walk to an Exxon station on Highway 19. It's pretty far away. It takes about thirty minutes to walk there.

We're definitely not supposed to be that far from Spring Meadow, but neither of us mentions that.

We have my one umbrella and I wouldn't mind squeezing together under it but it's not raining hard so Stewart pulls his hoodie over his head.

There's no streetlights out here in the country, so it's really dark, but our eyes get used to it enough to see the road. It's kind of cool actually: walking through the misty darkness, surrounded by the towering evergreen trees.

Thirty minutes later the Exxon station appears like an oasis in the gloom. It has a little Handy Mart, which we are in need of. I follow Stewart inside, where we find a hot-chocolate machine. We dig through our pockets for change. Then Stewart turns and walks right into a beer refrigerator. It's like an entire wall of beer. There's everything: six-packs, tall boys, forties, short cases, mini-kegs. You can smell that sour beer smell. You can feel the carbonation in your bones.

For a moment, both of us freeze in place. The guy working there is in a little booth, reading his newspaper. We could totally steal anything we want.

I see Stewart's whole body tighten up. Then he turns to me. Our eyes meet. We're both like, *Holy shit.*

Stewart hurriedly turns back to the hot-chocolate machine. I go to the counter and quickly pay for two hot chocolates.

A second later we're out of there.

Outside, there's no place to go, no place to sit. So we sit on the ground, huddled together, our backs against the side of the Handy Mart.

I can tell Stewart's a little shaken up.

"You okay?" I ask.

"Yeah."

"You looked like you saw a ghost in there."

"I kinda did."

We sip our hot chocolates. He lets his head rest back against the wall.

"Where are you from?" I ask him, changing the subject.

"Centralia."

"What's that like?"

"It's okay. Small town. How about you?"

"West Linn," I say. "I live with my parents."

"What's that like?"

"It's the suburbs. Nice houses. Nice cars. Kids on Ritalin."

"Sounds like fun."

I drink my hot chocolate. I look at the small silver ring on his pinkie.

"Nice ring," I say.

He looks at it, touches it. "It's my grandmother's."

"Huh," I say, secretly relieved.

"She died." He holds it closer to his face. "She used to look out for me. A lot more than my own parents."

He holds his hand toward me, so I can see the ring better. I take his cold fingers in mine. He has thick knuckles, dirty fingernails.

"She was the last thing holding me down," he says, taking his hand back. "After that I sorta lost it."

"It's a nice ring," I say. I drink my hot chocolate. We sit quietly for a while.

"So is this your first time in one of these places?" he asks, gesturing back toward Spring Meadow.

"Yeah."

"What do you think of it?"

"I dunno. I mostly complain."

"Do you believe all that stuff they say?" he asks. "You gotta change your whole life? Get new friends? Do everything different?"

"I guess," I say. I pick at my paper cup. "I didn't have that many friends to start with."

"Yeah. Me neither."

A slow winter wind sways the treetops beyond the Exxon station. A low swooshing sound fills the air. I snuggle a little closer to Stewart.

A pickup truck pulls into the gas station. A man in a yellow rain slicker gets out and starts pumping his gas. Stewart watches the man. I watch Stewart. He has the most interesting face. It is beautiful, young, almost childlike, and yet with a power and authority in his features. In another time, he would have been a young warrior, or a Lost Prince exiled from his kingdom. But he's from this time, this place, so he's just some "at-risk" kid who can't find a place for himself in the straight world.

• • •

We get up. We stand, stretch our legs, brush off our butts. We throw our empty cups in the trash, bumping into each other, our shoulders touching for a moment. We stay like that, touching.

Two of my fingers find their way into his coat pocket. His hand touches my shoulder. We pretend that it's the cold, we just need to get warm for a second. We move close and hug in an odd, "friends" way. But then we don't let go.

And then it changes to something else. A kind of exploration. Could we . . . ? Would we . . . ? We linger inside the question, holding each other, shifting our grips, trying it out. There is no rush, no hurry. There is no sense of time at all.

And then it changes again. To something more powerful. Something unstoppable. Like a wave in the ocean, pushing us, taking us somewhere. His face searches for me. His lips glance off my forehead, off my cheek. My whole body begins to tingle. He eases down farther, finds my mouth, kisses it.

He tastes like hot chocolate. His mouth is warm and silvery and milky and soft. It's just a kiss at first, but then slowly I let myself go, I lose myself in his face, his breath, the contours of his mouth.

When we finally separate, we are both overwhelmed and embarrassed. We retreat back under the shelter of the awning. But now I stay close to him, burrowing into that army coat, pressing against him for warmth.

We kiss again, this time with more force. We mash up against the glass window of the Handy Mart. His hands slip inside my coat and find the curves of my waist.

We kiss until we are out of breath, and then he breaks it off and laughs and without completely releasing me, steers us both into the rain.

We run, arm in arm, across the cement, through the gas pumps, and onto the empty road. We sprint, racing for a moment down the wet asphalt. Then we laugh and slow down, finally stopping to hold each other and make out some more under the gray, misting sky.

In this way, we return home. It takes forever but we are not cold anymore. We don't mind the rain. We laugh, skip, chase each other, nearly knock each other down. It's like we've entered a separate reality. Like now it's just the two of us, nothing else matters, no one else exists.

19

When I finally get home, the lights are off. I creep quietly up the steps, unlock the door, go inside. A single lamp is on in the front room. The bedrooms are all dark, everyone is in their bunks, asleep.

I go into the bathroom and strip out of my wet clothes. I towel off and then sneak quietly into my room, where I slip on some dry underwear and a T-shirt. Margarita stirs in the next bunk. I crawl into my own bed and burrow into my comforter.

This is where I want to be now, alone with myself. Because I know that something has happened to me tonight, something that I'm not going to understand at first, something I need to just absorb and think about and get used to.

This is going to be hard for me. I can't control this. I can't stop what it will do to me.

But I want it. I want to be inside it, to feel it, forever.

I turn to the wall. I hear the other people breathing around me, the creaking of the beds, the sound of the rain, falling harder now, outside on the window.

And then I feel something else. Something that's totally new. I feel the tiniest sensation of hope.

Maybe my life isn't over. Maybe my life has just begun.

20

"So I hear you had a little midnight frolic last night," says Cynthia the next day, glaring at me across her desk.

"What?" I say. "Who told you that?"

"There's a reason we have these rules, Madeline," she says forcefully. "And it's not just to protect you. It's to protect the other people as well."

"How did you —?" I stammer. "Who —?"

"You've been in the transition residency a month and a half!" she says, cutting me off. "This poor boy just got here. He's barely finished his twenty-eight days. Do you realize how vulnerable he is?"

I rise to the fight. "You're not allowed to spy on us. It's illegal!"

"Never mind that you're endangering your own sobriety. You are also endangering the sobriety of someone with less time and less experience than you have!"

"I can't believe you're lecturing me about this!" I shoot back. "First you tell me I have to have friends. Then you tell me who they're supposed to be. Now you tell me I can't go for a walk with a boy who I actually like? Who I actually care about?"

"So you care about him? Are you sure? Do you even know what that means?"

"Do you?" I snap. "Sitting there judging me? You're supposed to trust us. I thought that was the point of the halfway house, to let us make our own decisions. I got sent here to stop drinking. Not to get lectured on which people I can talk to . . ."

Cynthia sits back and watches me sputter and protest. When I'm done, she closes her notebook.

"The rules are the rules," she says. "If this happens again, you'll both be kicked out."

"It's ridiculous," I say. "And it's not fair!"

"No, Maddie. It's more than fair. If you're not going to take this seriously then you should get out and make room for someone who will. People die because they can't get in here."

"People don't *die*."

"Oh, they don't? Says you? Who knows so much? You don't know how lucky you are, Madeline. And all I can hope is that you survive long enough to figure that out!"

go to movie night on Tuesday. Stewart is there. He sits next to me in the backseat. He doesn't talk. Neither do I.

"Did you get yelled at?" I finally ask.

"A little bit," he says.

"Sorry about that."

"It's not your fault."

We kind of smile at each other then. I creep my hand across the seat and hold his hand while the van drives.

At The Carlton, I buy us two popcorns and we sit with the other rehab people. We don't do anything. We watch the movie. It's enough to be close. We touch forearms and hold hands a little.

On the van ride back, though, I want to hold him so badly. It gets sort of impossible. It's worse than craving alcohol. I want him like I've never wanted a boy before.

I close my eyes and wait for it to pass. Which sorta works. But sorta doesn't.

Two days later, Stewart comes to the laundry room. He comes during lunch and knocks quietly on the back door. When I see who it is, I can barely contain myself. I yank the door open and pull him inside.

He's wearing his maintenance crew coveralls and a baseball hat. He's acting shy and looking at the ground.

"I don't think I'm supposed to come in here," he says.

"You can come in here," I say defiantly. "You can come in here any time you want."

I grab him and hug him, despite the fact that it's broad daylight and Rami, the laundry room boss, is right in the next room.

His face turns red when I do this. He steps back from me and looks around the laundry room. "So this is where you work?"

I nod.

"Those are big washing machines."

"There's a lot of stuff to wash."

He takes off his baseball cap and looks down at the floor. "I just wanted to apologize again for getting you into trouble."

"You didn't get me in trouble," I say, watching his face. "I got you in trouble. And I'm sorry. I'm so sorry." I take his hand and kiss it.

"It was my fault," he says, taking his hand back. "I'm older. I'm the guy. I should know better."

"That's ridiculous!" I whisper. "The rule is ridiculous. What do they want from us anyway?"

"I know," he says. "But they must have their reasons."

"I don't care about their reasons. If we want to be together, they can't stop us!"

He says nothing. He doesn't look up.

"Don't you want to be together?" I say.

"Well, yeah, but not if it gets us kicked out."

I'm about to explode. I want to rant against stupid

Spring Meadow and all their idiotic rules. But that might freak Stewart out. So I don't. I do the opposite. I try to calm myself down.

"Okay," I say, taking a breath. "Maybe you're right. Maybe I'm . . . being selfish. Of course we want to hang out. We just can't right now."

"It's not forever," he says. "I mean, how long until you're out of here?"

"Two more weeks."

"And I got another month after that. So we just gotta wait a little. We just gotta be patient."

I nod my agreement, even though I am so pissed.

"And there's still movie night," he says.

There's a noise from the other room. Rami is about to come in. Stewart jerks his hat back on and I walk him quickly to the back door. I want to kiss him but there's no time. He slips away at the last possible second.

22

At movie night the next week, Stewart and I are both thinking the same thing. We buy our tickets, stand around in the lobby, get our popcorn, then linger near the theater doors while the other people sit.

Then we bail.

Outside, I want to grab him, kiss him. Somehow I restrain myself.

We walk all the way to the other end of Carlton, to the Denny's. We go inside and sit at the counter and get hot chocolates. This will be "our" drink, we decide. I actually decide this, but he goes along.

Afterward, in the parking lot, we find a dark place to make out. We really get into it. When we head back to the theater I am light-headed and dizzy. I cling to Stewart in case my weak knees give out.

In the van, we sit in the backseat. We sit close. The lust is gone and now I just hold his arm and — when nobody's looking — lean against him and rest my head against his shoulder.

That night in my bunk, I can still smell him on my sweater. I take it off and carefully spread it over my pillow and breathe each section of it, trying to find him, trying to keep him near, holding him in my mind until the last possible moment.

23

On my last Tuesday at Spring Meadow, Stewart and I go to movie night and do our bailing trick, skipping out the back of the theater. We return to the same Denny's, but this time we're not all giddy and excited. This is it. This is our last night together, at least here in Carlton. We order hot chocolates.

We talk on and off. Nothing profound. He tells me about his adventures trying to take a class in motorcycle mechanics at community college. His grandmother kept giving him money and somehow, with the best of intentions, he always ended up buying drugs.

We laugh at the predictability of it. I tell him about a group of us crashing a junior prom so high on OxyContin we could barely stand up and how the chaperones stopped us and thought we were drunk. So we told them that our friend had one leg that was shorter than the other, and that's why she couldn't walk straight. And they believed us!

Stewart chuckles at this. We drink our hot chocolate.

"You'll probably go to a real college," he says.

"Me?" I say. "No way. I probably won't even graduate from high school."

"Yeah, you will," he says.

"What about you?" I say. "You could go to college. Now that you're sober."

"I kinda doubt it."

"Why not?" I say. "You're smart. You can go to community college for a year and then transfer."

"Yeah, maybe."

This is a difficult conversation and I'm glad when we change the subject. Later, when he goes to the restroom, I look out the window. *Stewart could totally go to college*, I tell myself. *He'll just need help.*

In the van, I ask Stewart if he wants to try to meet later that night. Since we only have two days left. Like maybe one of us could sneak over to the other's house.

He shakes his head no.

He's right of course. I feel bad I even suggested it.

"Okay, then," I whisper, close to his ear. "I'll be like one of those prison girlfriends. Waiting for you on the outside. Dreaming about you every night."

He shakes his head, grins, then kisses me on the temple.

24

The day before I leave, Stewart comes to the laundry room. He knocks on the back door. I let him in and I kind of lose it for a second, like I can't quite breathe. I have been thinking about him every second of these last days.

But then he acts weird and standoffish. He stays by the door. He's being shy. I want him to look at me, to hold me. This is the last time I'm going to see him for five weeks!

"You excited about leaving?" he finally says.

"Not really," I say, a panic building in my chest.

"Why not?" he says.

"Why do you think!?" I say to him. "God!"

"Are you talking about me?"

"Of course I'm talking about you!" I cry. "I'm not going to see you for a month!" Tears spring to my eyes. "What am I supposed to do on Tuesday night? Who am I supposed to drink hot chocolate with?"

He looks embarrassed.

"What about you?" I ask him. "Are *you* glad I'm leaving?"

"No. Of course I'm not. But I'm glad for you."

We both stand there, looking at the floor. One of the washing machines switches to spin cycle. It starts to shake.

"Are you going to stay sober?" he asks in a careful voice.

"*Yes*. I was planning on it. Are you?"

"Yeah."

"Are you gonna call me?" I ask him.

"Sure."

"You better! God!"

"I will," he says. "Of course I will."

I can't stand it anymore. I grab him. A sob bursts out of my chest. Stewart takes me in his arms.

"It's okay," he tells me, rocking me.

"I'm afraid," I whisper. "I'm afraid it won't be the same after we leave here. Something will happen. Something will change."

He strokes my hair. "Of course things will change. But it'll work out."

"I don't know how to do this," I say, clutching him. "I don't know how to lose someone."

"You're not losing anyone," he says, releasing me. "In fact, I want to give you something."

He takes his grandmother's ring off his little finger.

I wipe the tears from my eyes. "You can't give me that," I say.

"I'm just lending it to you. I want you to hold it for me."

"I . . . I can't —"

"See if it fits."

I take the ring. I look at it. I try putting it on my ring finger. It fits perfectly.

"But what if I lose it?"

"Don't lose it."

"But I always lose stuff."

He closes my hand around the ring. "When I get out of here, you can give it back," he says. "And in the meantime it'll protect you, like it's protected me."

"But I —"

There's a noise in the next room. Rami's back from lunch. "I better go," Stewart says.

I throw my arms around him and squeeze him with all my strength. He hugs me back, for one second, then two. Then stupid Rami starts whistling in the other room. That means he's about to come in. Stewart pulls away and slips out without a sound. I stand there, staring at the closed door.

Rami comes in. He continues to whistle as he checks the dryers.

I look down at the ring. I turn it on my finger.

part two

My mom waits her turn in the morning traffic jam in front of my high school. I sit in the passenger seat with my book bag in my lap, staring at the green grass, the stone steps, the front doors. I can't believe I'm doing this. I can't believe I am back at Evergreen High School.

"Do you have everything?" Mom asks.

"I think so," I say.

I get out of the car. I sling my book bag over my shoulder. I'm dressed as boringly as humanly possible. Since it's January, that means down coat, Levi's, black Converse. My hair's pulled back. No makeup. No lip gloss. Nothing.

I keep my eyes down as I trudge across the grass. I heave my backpack farther up my shoulder. I'm loaded up with textbooks. There will be a lot of catching up to do. My teachers better cut me some slack in that department. But of course they will. Everyone knows what the deal is. Everyone understands that Madeline Graham is officially getting her second chance.

• • •

I make it to the main building. I'm totally aware of the people on the stairs around me. Are they watching me? Talking about me? Do people stop what they're doing when I pass?

No. Not really.

Homeroom is different, though. Every eye is on me, from the minute I walk in the door. I move through my staring classmates and take my usual place in the back of the room. Then I remember that I have been instructed to never sit in the back of classrooms, to never sit in the back of any room. (Too antisocial; I am supposed to participate.) So I go to the middle of the room, but that feels too claustrophobic. So I go to the side of the room, by the window, and take a seat there, next to a boy I don't know. He's one of those keep-your-head-down types, which is probably what I'll turn into.

I sit. I dig out my new monthly organizer that my mother bought me. On the top there's a note:

Dear Maddie,
A new year, a new start.
Love, Mom

I draw a box around the note, I draw several boxes. More people come in. I don't look up.

Then a loud voice bellows at me from behind. "Maddie Graham!? Is that you!?"

It's Tara Peterson, the biggest dork in our school. She's standing right over me.

"Yes, it's me," I say.

"Have you been sick?" asks Tara loudly. "Where have you been?"

I look up at her, I give her my best "please don't do this" smile.

But people like Tara don't understand things like hints.

"Did you have mono?" she asks me.

"No."

"Where were you, then?"

"I was . . ." I see that other people are watching us. They're listening to what I'm going to say. Even the head-down boy next to me has turned to hear my answer.

"I had a family situation," I say.

"Oh my gawd!" she says at maximum volume. "Did somebody die?"

"No, nobody died."

"It must have been bad, though. You've been gone for months!"

"All right, class! Everyone in your seats," says Mrs. Wagner, our teacher. Thank God.

2

Lunch is going to be a problem, but I have a plan. I eat a little bit at every period break. I do this secretly, hiding the snacks in my locker. I eat baby carrots, half a sandwich, some celery with peanut butter. Then during the actual lunch period, I go to the library. I find the cross-word puzzle in the day's newspaper and take it to the back table, laying it out beside my history book and pretending it's my homework.

It's a pleasant way to spend forty minutes.

Things get more difficult after lunch, though, when Emily Brantley spots me in the breezeway.

"Hey, Rehab Girl!" she yells out.

I act like I don't know who she's talking to. I walk faster.

But she runs after me. "Don't try to ignore me," she says loudly.

I keep walking. Emily's one of the cool girls in our school. We were never really friends, though we hung out with some of the same people. We were more like rivals.

She runs after me. "Hey," she says, catching up. "So how was it?"

"How was what?"

"You know," she says. "Rehab."

"What do you care?"

"I'm just curious," she says. "You don't have to get snippy."

"And you didn't have to call me Rehab Girl in front of the whole breezeway."

"Nobody cares. And it's not like it's a big secret."

I keep walking. She walks with me. "So are you really going to do it?" she asks.

"Do what?"

"Stay on the straight and narrow."

"I don't know. I guess we'll find out."

"Well, good luck," she says. "It won't be easy. Not around here."

I look at her. She appears to be sincere, which is a surprise.

"And if you decide to step off the wagon, you know where the good stuff is," she says, slapping her coat pocket.

"Thanks a lot," I say.

She laughs. "Dude. I'm kidding! Seriously, I wish you luck. I mean it. I'll probably end up in there myself someday!"

Despite all this, Emily's not my biggest social problem.

That would be my three best friends: Jake, Raj, and Alex. They're the ones who will test my resolve.

Jake appears at my locker before sixth period. I take a deep breath when I see him waiting for me.

"Hey, you're back," he says in his totally cute, totally casual voice.

"Yeah."

"So how was it?"

"It sucked," I say.

"Yeah, I guess it would."

I suddenly get really nervous. Like my hands start to shake and my throat kind of tightens up in some way.

Jake doesn't notice. He's totally chill, as always. He leans against the locker next to mine.

"So what happens in there?" he asks.

"Nothing. They just order you around a lot."

"Huh," he says, staring blankly down the hall. "So are you, like, finished now? Free and clear?"

"I don't have to go back, if that's what you mean."

"Huh. So that means you can come get high with us after school?"

"Well. No."

"So you're actually going to do it? You're actually gonna quit?"

"Yeah," I say, sighing. "I think I am. For now."

Jake nods. "That's too bad," he says. "Raj just got some killer Colombian. He was psyched to smoke you out. You know, like, to welcome you back." As he says this, he sort of leans toward me, doing his sexy Jake thing.

"I don't think I better. Sorry."

Jake shrugs. "So what are you gonna do? I mean, if you can't hang out?"

"I don't know. Crawl in a hole, I guess."

"That sucks."

"I know."

"Huh," he says. At that moment, Marisa Petrovich walks by. She's wearing a very short skirt. "Hey, Marisa," he calls out.

"Hey, *Jake*," she purrs.

"All right, then," he says to me. "I'll see you around, I guess."

"Tell Raj thanks," I say. "You know, for thinking of me."

"No worries." Jake's now staring at a slutty sophomore I don't know. Her top is cut so low she's basically showing the world her tits. Jake practically falls over trying to look at them.

Oh yeah, high school, I think to myself. *This is a great idea.*

3

My whole first week is like that. People coming up to me. Asking me polite questions. Then avoiding me like the plague. It's excruciating.

Stewart calls from Spring Meadow, but he can only talk for ten minutes. Somehow we can't seem to keep the conversation going. It's still nice. But also weirdly frustrating.

On Friday night my mother drives me to a Teens at Risk support group Dr. Bernstein runs. There's, like, eight of us. We go around the room and talk about our "issues." These are mostly rich girls from my neighborhood. It's not that their problems aren't real. It's just so tedious the way they talk about them. It's all therapy-speak and *my wants* and *my needs* and *me, me, me.*

At least the people at rehab were funny. At least Vern always had good dirty jokes.

Halfway through, I can't stand it anymore and I bail. I go outside and sit on the cement steps in the cold. The social worker woman comes out and tries to talk to me, and I'm like: "I'm fine, really I am. I just can't deal with this right now."

So she goes back inside and I put my head down on my knees and I ask God to just kill me, I can't take this. I can't live like this. School is impossible. I have a semester's worth of homework to make up. I have no friends. I have nothing to do, nowhere to go, no one to talk to.

No wonder Vern gets drunk every year.

4

Another week passes, and then one night at dinner my dad hands me a gift-wrapped box. It's a present. I open it and it's a new phone. This is a little risky since I'm famous for losing cell phones. Or dropping them in toilets. Or throwing them at cops.

They make a big deal of giving it to me, congratulating me on a job well done. My dad tells me I'm doing great, everyone is so proud of me. He says he feels like he's got his old Maddie back.

I have no idea what that means, since all I do is walk around in a suicidal haze. But whatever. I thank them politely and escape upstairs to my room as soon as I can. I don't know who to call exactly. I'm not allowed to call Stewart after six at the halfway house. I can't really call Jake or Raj. There's no one else I can think of.

But then I remember someone.

I dig through my desk and find a certain scrap of paper. Trish's number. I haven't called her since she left Spring Meadow. I guess I haven't been desperate enough. I'm desperate enough now.

I put her number in and dial it.

It rings. I wait. I get nervous in my stomach.

"Hello?" says a sleepy voice.

"Hello?" I say. "Is this Trish?"

"Who's this?"

"Maddie."

"Maddie?" The voice seems to wake up slightly. "Maddie from Spring Meadow?"

"Yes! Trish! It's me!"

"Oh my God. It's you?" she says. "Where are you!?"

"I'm home!"

"Oh my God! When did you get out?" she asks excitedly. "What are you doing?"

"I'm living with my parents. I'm back in high school!"

"You're back in high school!? How weird! What's it like? Does it suck?"

"Are you kidding me? It totally sucks!"

"Oh my God! You're in high school! That's hilarious!"

"I know. It's a total joke!"

"I'm so glad you called!" she says.

"Me too!"

"It's so nice to hear your voice!"

"What have you been doing?"

"I've been applying for jobs. My mom is making me. I applied for a bookkeeper at a plumbing company. Can you imagine me? Working at a plumbing company!?"

"That is so funny!!!"

"It's ridiculous!"

"We have to hang out."

"We totally have to."

"Oh my God, I can't wait to see you!"

"What are you doing tomorrow?"

"I'm coming to see you!!!"

· · ·

The next day I ride the MAX train downtown, to the Metro Café. That's the cool place downtown where people hang out.

I walk in and see Trish sitting by herself in a corner. We wave and I hurry through the tables to her. I sit down and we gush and hold hands and act stupid for a while. Then we get lattes and settle in with each other.

She looks different. That's the first thing I notice. She's gained weight and is wearing different makeup. She has a new expensive haircut that looks weird, like it's really intended for a fifty-year-old woman who works in a bank. Also, she looks kind of asleep. Or puffy. She's on meds, obviously. Pretty massive doses, from the looks of her.

But none of this makes any difference. Once we're talking, it's just like back at rehab. It's just like old times. She has crushes on a million different guys. A guy she liked in high school called her last week. She went to an AA meeting where there were some cute skater boys. She flirts with one of the cashiers at the grocery store by her mom's.

I tell her about school. How I hide in the library and eat carrots all day and do crossword puzzles at lunch.

"Oh my God, could we be bigger losers!!??" She laughs.

After coffee we walk around downtown. This is the best hour I've spent in weeks. We laugh at stuff for no reason. We joke about jobs and school. We walk arm in arm and say random things to boys.

There's just one thing: I don't tell her about Stewart. I don't know why. I start to a couple times. But then I don't.

For some reason I need to keep him to myself.

5

Having Trish back in my life makes everything more tolerable. School gets easier. My parents don't seem so weird. Even talking to Stewart gets easier, as it gives me something to talk about for our whole ten minutes.

It goes so well, in fact, that he calls me again the next day. I'm in the kitchen with my mom when I answer. She gets sort of weird and suspicious afterward, which is odd, considering all the stray boys who have called me over the years. She wants to know who he is, and I tell her he's one of my friends from rehab. I remind her we're supposed to maintain friendships with our fellow recoverers. She doesn't totally understand the "recovery" philosophy but she takes my word for it. Sort of.

Then he calls again a couple days later on a borrowed cell phone. It's a Saturday, early afternoon, and I'm alone at home and I wander around the house half naked in a big sweater, talking to him for two hours. We have a real talk this time. We make plans. He's going to stay with his mother in Centralia, which is about fifty miles from Portland. I can come visit him there. And he can come into the city.

He gives me the news from Spring Meadow: who's been going to movie night, what's going on in his house, how he played cards with Rami the other day and how he's sorta nice, he even knew we were together in the laundry room those times but didn't tell anyone.

Hearing about Spring Meadow brings tears to my eyes. Or maybe it's just having such a nice long talk with Stewart. After I hang up, I lie on my bed in my sweater. I know it will probably be weird when he gets out. Of course it will be. And he's so cute, and so helpless, every girl he meets is going to fall in love with him.

This is not going to be easy, whatever happens between us. But I let myself love him anyway. I let myself love him with all my heart. I give myself that. I tell myself I deserve it.

So *that's* where the crossword puzzle has been hiding!"

I open my eyes. I've fallen asleep on the couch in the back of the library. My textbook is in my lap with the unfinished crossword puzzle tucked inside it.

A boy I don't know snatches it away and takes it to the table. "And you're the one who gets them all wrong."

"I don't get them all wrong," I say, blinking myself awake and sitting up straight.

"You're not supposed to sleep in the library," he says.

"I'm not sleeping. I'm resting."

"You should photocopy these puzzles, if you're gonna mess them up so bad."

"Who are you?" I say, staring at this utterly obnoxious boy.

"Martin Farris. You should know that. We're in Yearbook together."

"Right. Yearbook," I say, Yearbook being the easiest, dumbest extracurricular there is at our school. I sleep in there a bit too.

Martin begins reading through the clues I've filled in. "You don't know who Jimi Hendrix is?" he asks. "Nineteen Down? Purple Haze composer?"

"I don't listen to classic rock."

"You should still know that. Jimi Hendrix was from Seattle."

"What difference does that make?"

"It's called *knowing about music that's from your area*? Like if you lived in Liverpool you would probably know of a little band called the Beatles?"

"You're kidding, right?"

He goes back to the crossword: "And Turkey's capital city is *Ankara*," he says. "Not 'ankle', or whatever it was you were trying to write."

I stare at him. "Look at you. You're like a total dork."

"I'm not a dork. I'm a geek," says Martin without hesitating. "Dorks are physically uncoordinated. Geeks have specialized knowledge of complex systems."

"Wow," I say.

"So where did you transfer from?" says Martin, still studying my crossword failures.

"I'm not a transfer."

"You weren't here last semester."

"Yes, I was."

"No, you weren't," he says. "I happen to work on Yearbook. I know who was here and who wasn't."

"I took some time off."

"What for?"

"Personal reasons."

"What sort of personal reasons?" he asks.

"None of your business."

He pretends to think: "Well . . . let's see . . . personal reasons. That could be health. That could be psychological issues.
Maybe you were impregnated by Satan and had to give birth to
your demon child in a secret location. . . ."

"You're hilarious," I say. I gather my stuff, since the bell is
about to ring.

He continues to cruise through the puzzle. "Twenty-two
down. Kind of guard. *Point,*" he says, writing it in.

I stand up with my backpack. "Thanks a lot, nerd boy,"
I say.

"No prob," he says, without looking up. "See you in
Yearbook."

call Cynthia a few days later, for one of our scheduled follow-up conversations. She's impressed I'm still alive.

I give her the lowdown: I'm sleeping better. I'm not really craving anything. I'm going to Dr. Bernstein's Teens at Risk support group, which I hate. Besides that, I go to school. I come home and watch TV. I hang out with Trish on weekends, (which amuses Cynthia to no end). She sounds pleased with my progress but tells me I need to go to AA meetings.

So I call Trish the next day and the two of us venture to a so-called "Young People's" AA meeting.

Trish's mom drives us in the Cadillac Escalade. It's in the basement of an old stone church. We go inside. Not everyone there is actually young, but most are. It's a boisterous crowd. People have tattoos, weird hair, piercings. Trish finds us seats along the wall.

There are some cute boys. That's why Trish likes it. The two in front of us roll their skateboards back and forth under their chairs. They look like hardened criminals to me, but Trish is drooling over them. She's all sexed up tonight, wearing super-tight jeans and thick, black eye makeup that looks a little scary with her puffy face and multiple layers of foundation.

She looks terrible, to be honest. So do I, but I know enough to wear baggy clothes and keep my eyes to myself.

So we sit there and they do the whole AA routine. I remember it from rehab. It gets boring, though, and Trish can't sit still and so halfway through we sneak out to the parking lot so she can smoke.

We stand in the cold, under the parking lot lights. Trish blows tight streams of smoke into the sky.

"If I don't get laid, I'm gonna lose my mind," Trish tells me.

I nod.

"Do you ever feel like that?" she says. "Or am I just insane?"

"Yeah, I feel like that."

"How could you, though? You don't even like any boys."

"Yeah, I do."

"Like who? Name one."

"This one guy."

"What guy? A guy you haven't told me about?"

"Yeah. Kinda."

"Really?" she says, smoking. "Where did you meet him?"

"I met him a while ago."

"Where?"

"At Spring Meadow," I say guiltily.

"Spring Meadow?"

"It was after you left."

Trish glares at me. "You met a guy at Spring Meadow?"

"Not there. At the halfway house. After you left."

"And you like this guy? For real?"

I nod.

"Why didn't you tell me this?"

"I don't know," I say, shrugging. "No reason."

"Were you hiding it?"

"No. I was just, you know, trying to keep it . . . low-key."

"Keep what low-key? Did you do it with him?"

"No. Well . . . we fooled around a little. . . ."

"You *fooled around* with a guy at Spring Meadow?" says Trish. "Jesus, Madeline. Do you still talk to him?"

"Yeah."

"And when were you planning on telling me this?"

"I don't know."

"That feels really weird to me. You know?" She turns away. She's pissed. "You got with some guy? And you're not saying a word about it? And meanwhile I'm slutting around, making a fool of myself? And you're keeping your little secret romance to yourself?"

"It's not like that."

"Well, what's it like, then? How could you not tell me?"

"It's just. I think I love him."

"And I don't love people?"

"I don't know. You're more into . . . sex."

"And you're not?"

I look up at the sky.

"I can't believe this," she says, grinding her cigarette out on the dirty asphalt. "You've been holding out on me. This whole time. Keeping your pure love away from slutty Trish. I can't believe this. You think you're better than me, don't you?"

"No."

"You do. You totally do."

"C'mon, Trish. . . ."

"And you're supposed to be my friend."

"I am your friend, Trish," I say.

"Y*ou better wake up*," whispers a voice.

Someone bumps against my shoulder and I snap my head up. I'm sitting at a table, surrounded by Yearbook dorks.

Martin Farris is beside me.

"Is the teacher here?" I ask.

"No."

I refocus my eyes. "Then why did you wake me up?"

"Because you're gonna fall off your chair."

"I happen to be good at sleeping in chairs."

Martin goes back to his fascinating freshman swim team article.

"Why are you sitting next to me?" I ask him.

"There was no place else to sit."

When Yearbook lets out, I can't get out of there fast enough. I can't lose Martin, though. For some reason he follows me down the hall.

"So . . . I . . . uh . . ." Martin says to me in a voice that is not his usual overconfident, robot dork voice.

"So you what?" I say back.

"I asked my friend Kaitlyn about you."

"Yeah?"

"I asked her where you might have been last semester. She said you were in rehab."

"That's right," I say, walking a little faster.

"She laughed at me. She said everyone in the whole school knew about it, and why was I so stupid?"

"That's kind of what I thought too," I say.

"And then I started thinking about it," he says, trying to keep up. "And it all made sense. That's why you go to the library. Because you used to hang out with Jake and Raj and those guys. But they usually skip out and smoke weed during lunch, so you go to the library and do the crossword puzzle and sleep."

"Good work, detective," I say.

"So then I was thinking you probably don't have anything to do on weekends, or anytime really, and maybe I should offer to do something with you."

I keep walking.

"Not anything big," he continues. "Just like, maybe you need someone to hang out with. Or go somewhere with. Or something like that."

"And you were going to volunteer yourself for this duty?"

"Sure. Why not? We could go to the mall. Go ice-skating or whatever. It's not like I've got that much going on right now."

"No kidding? A cool dude like you has nothing going on?"

He frowns at this but continues his speech. "I just thought I should offer. It was Kaitlyn who suggested ice-skating."

"Ice-skating?"

"Yeah. She said girls like that."

"God, you really are a dork."

"Or a movie. Or whatever."

"And this wouldn't be a date?"

"Not at all. It would just be . . . helping you out. A good deed. Because you probably don't have any non-stoner friends. Obviously you don't. You probably don't have *any* friends now, if what Kaitlyn said is true."

"So you're offering yourself as a dork-replacement-friend sort of thing."

"No. Actually, I don't think I would want to be your real friend. You're not very nice. But I could spare a little time to help someone, you know, in a difficult situation."

"How thoughtful of you."

"It *is* thoughtful of me. I just . . . we could even just sit around and do crossword puzzles if you wanted."

"No offense," I say, veering away from him, toward the parking lot. "But that sounds like the worst idea ever."

But in fact, doing crossword puzzles with Martin is not the worst idea ever.

The worst idea ever is going with Trish to the hospital to visit her ex–best friend, who is paralyzed.

I'd agreed to this before our little fight. And now that Trish has guilt-leverage on me, there's no escape.

My mom has to drive us, because Trish's Cadillac is in the shop. I explain to my mom it's a "recovery" errand, that going to see the person Trish crippled in a drunk-driving accident is the responsible thing to do. Mom is pretty freaked out by the idea. So am I. But we go.

We pick up Trish at her house and drive across town to Providence Hospital. Of course I have been telling my mom that Trish is a really important friend and is super nice and normal and not screwed up at all.

When my mom sees Trish in person, with her swollen face and her bizarre haircut, she is slightly horrified.

But she says nothing. That's one thing about my family. We have good manners.

My mom drops us off at the hospital and we go in. Trish

wants to get a bunch of candy at the little store inside. So we wait in line and get a huge box of Hot Tamales and Mike and Ikes and Jujubes and stuff like that.

"Haley likes Hot Tamales," she tells me. Then she opens the Jujubes and starts eating them herself. She eats a couple at a time. Her mouth fills up with them.

We walk deeper into the hospital. Trish knows the way. It's creepy walking down the long hallways. There's no windows, no air. Trish isn't bothered. She's being her usual flighty self, walking too fast and not paying attention to where she's going, or who she's knocking into, unless it's a cute doctor, or any other guy between the ages of fifteen and forty-five.

We ride the elevator to the eleventh floor. Trish is downing the Jujubes. I've never seen someone stuff so much candy in her face. It's scary and it makes me nervous about what's to come.

The elevator door opens. We get off. We walk down the hall. Trish is moving very fast now. I have to run to keep up.

We get to Haley's room and Trish goes barging in, but the room is empty, the bed is empty.

"I know where she is," says Trish, pushing me aside and continuing our frantic march down the hall. We come around the corner and there she is, in her wheelchair, a meek-looking blond girl with a small, sad face. She is just sitting in the hall, doing nothing. The look in her eyes, when she sees us, is of deep fear.

"Hey, Haley," says Trish, talking about as fast as a human can talk. "This is Madeline, the girl I told you about? We lived together in the halfway house? We're friends and we hang out, because we're both sober now and drug free and we're supposed to be friends with other sober people so that's what we do. She's very nice and she's smart like you and gets good grades and I think you guys will really hit it off. I brought you these too, Hot Tamales, I know you like them, I know they're your favorite. I also got Mike and Ikes, the fruity ones. And some Jujubes."

At this point, Trish grabs my arm and yanks me forward.

I step up to the wheelchair and reach out my hand. But Haley can't lift her hands. She's paralyzed from the neck down.

I drop my hand. Haley stares up at me. Her face is the saddest thing I have ever seen.

A nurse comes around the corner. She hurries toward us. She doesn't look happy to see Trish. "You girls are a little late, aren't you? Visiting hours are over."

"I wanted Haley to meet my friend Madeline," says Trish. "I think they'll really hit it off. They're both sort of the same type and they'll probably be great friends. Won't you, Maddie? You like Haley, don't you? You guys could, like, play chess on the computer or something."

Trish is losing her shit. She can't stop talking. "I can't play chess at all. I'm terrible at games. But Haley's good at things like that, aren't you, Haley? You used to love Chutes and Ladders when we were kids. And Monopoly. You always wanted to play that. I always got bored playing board games. I just can't sit still, I guess."

The nurse grasps the handles of Haley's wheelchair and backs her away from us. She does not look happy with Trish.

"Can you feed her these Hot Tamales?" says Trish abruptly, trying to hand the box to the nurse. "She really likes them."

When the nurse doesn't take them, Trish lays the box on the front tray on Haley's wheelchair.

I suddenly realize that the nurse considers Trish a crazy person. Haley does too. The nurse wheels Haley away, leaving me and Trish standing alone in the hallway.

In the elevator, Trish can't speak. When the door opens, she takes off through the lobby, practically running toward the exit. I run to catch up, and when I do, she stops suddenly, turns, and collapses into a chair by the door. She lowers her head and starts rocking back and forth. I don't know what she's doing, but I sit down too, I put my hand on her back to calm her.

"Oh my God, oh my God, oh my God," she moans to herself. She curls up into herself, pulling her fists inside her sleeves.

"It's okay, Trish."

"Do you see now?" she says, her face bent down almost to her knees. "Do you see now what I'm talking about?"

"Yes," I say, though I don't really.

"I did that. I *did that*," she says to the ground. "And people want me to get a job? They want me to move forward with my life?" She covers her ears with her wrists.

"It's okay," I tell her.

"I just wanna be dead," she whispers into the carpet. "I do. It's all I ever wanted. I don't want to be here. I swear I don't."

Then she jumps up and runs out the door. I watch her disappear. I have no idea where she's going.

I dig my phone out and text my mom that we might be a while.

10

Two days later I'm riding in Martin Farris's car. We're going to the mall. I have apparently decided to let him be my dork-replacement-friend.

Martin parks in the underground parking lot and we go inside. He's dressed up a bit. He's wearing new, uncool Nikes, uncool jeans, and some sort of golf shirt.

We walk along the main concourse. It's a Friday night. Martin wanted to come on a weekend night because he thought weekend nights were probably the hardest for me.

"That's probably when you partied the most," he said on the phone.

"That's right," I said back, though in fact I "partied" about the same every night.

We cruise the mall. There are other people milling around. People on dates. It's pretty embarrassing, but I follow Martin around, like girls are supposed to. That's how I live now. I do what I'm supposed to do.

Martin steers us to the Cineplex. We look at the movie times and study the possibilities. One of the other movies finishes and a stream of people come out.

Suddenly, all I can think of is Stewart. The two of us slouched in the back of The Carlton theater, our feet draped over the seats.

And then I know I can't do this. No movies. Not with Martin Farris.

"I don't think I want to see a movie," I say.

"You don't? Why not?"

"Because."

Martin is confused. And a little hurt. "I thought that's why we came here?"

I avoid meeting his eye.

"Is it because you're with me?" he asks. "Because this isn't a date. I know that. Not at all."

"I just don't want to," I say. "I want to do something else. I want to go ice-skating."

"But you said you hated ice-skating."

"I want to try it," I lie, "I think it sounds like fun."

Martin leads us down the escalator to the ice rink. I don't know how to ice-skate. I've never even *thought* about ice-skating before.

We rent skates. We sit together on a wood bench and put them on. Martin is not speaking to me now. I've hurt his feelings. I should probably apologize. Or maybe he just needs to get over himself. He is a geek, after all. He said so himself.

With our skates on, we stand at the edge of the rink. I like the way the ice looks: perfectly flat, perfectly white. I like the bracing cold of it.

Martin is smart enough to know I don't want help, I don't want any hand-holding or other physical contact. So he leaves me to fend for myself.

I take my first cautious steps onto the ice. I think I'm going to take off and go flying around the rink like the other people, but in fact, the minute I step forward, I fall. And then I can't get up. And when I do, I fall again.

It's the skate blades. They bend over to the side. I stand up and try again and I fall backward this time, hard, on my ass.

Meanwhile, Martin has already glided off into the flow of the other people. He's totally skating.

I crawl to the wall and pull myself up. He completes a lap and comes up behind me.

"Jesus, Martin," I say. "How do you do this?"

"You have to hold your ankles straight," he says.

"How do you do *that*?"

"You have to flex your muscles a certain way."

He offers his arm and I hold on to it. I try again. I get a little speed going and then I fall again. I slide a few feet and then stop, sprawled on my back on the ice.

"This isn't fun," I say. "Why do people think this is fun?"

Martin helps me up and I try again, complaining bitterly the whole time, though the truth is, I don't mind it that much: falling, sliding to a stop, lying there on the cold whiteness.

It numbs me. Which I like.

Afterward, we go back to Martin's car. We pull out of the Lloyd Center parking lot.

"I guess we should head home," says Martin.

"We don't have to," I say. "It's only nine thirty."

"Yeah, but what are we going to do?"

"Let's go downtown," I say.

"What's downtown?"

"Life, Martin. The world."

We drive over the bridge into the city. Martin doesn't know anything about downtown. I have to tell him how to get there, what streets to take, where the cool places are.

We drive by Pioneer Courthouse Square, which is where the street kids hang out. I used to hang out there myself on occasion. I see some people I know standing around the MAX station. I see Jeff Weed, one of the local pot dealers, in a trench coat that has the word SUBHUMAN spray-painted on the back of it.

"See that guy?" I tell Martin. "That's Jeff Weed."

"Is that his real name?" Martin says, gawking out his window.

"And there's Bad Samantha."

Martin can't believe I know these people. He stares at them like they are aliens from outer space. "Are these the people who gave you drugs?"

"They don't give you drugs," I say. "You have to buy them."

I direct Martin to a different block and we park. As amusing as it is to watch Martin geek out, I feel a little unsettled myself. What if Jeff Weed tries to talk to me? What if Bad Samantha recognizes me? We almost got in a fight two summers ago.

I keep my head down as we slip inside the Metro Café.

Martin is not prepared for this scene either. He didn't know that young people actually go places other than Math Club or their next-door neighbors' basement to play video games. He doesn't know what to make of the stylish downtown girls. Or the cool skater dudes.

He orders a decaf latte. I get a triple espresso. I make him pay, and we find a table in the back and sit there, not talking. Martin mostly stares at people: two sexy girls in miniskirts, a boy wearing makeup. At one point, a loud, drunk girl wanders in and starts kicking someone. Her friends try to restrain her and she kicks them too. A manager appears and tries to wrestle her out the door.

"See that girl?" I say to Martin, sipping my espresso.

"Yeah?"

"That was me."

When he drops me off at home, Martin thanks me for taking him downtown.

"You can go there yourself, you know," I tell him.

"I don't think I'd go there myself. But I'm glad I went."

I get out. I look back at Martin as I close the car door. He's staring out the windshield thinking about everything he just saw. He's probably realizing for the first time how utterly clueless and sheltered he is.

"Night, Martin," I say.

"Yeah," he says. "Okay. Night."

I wave and walk up my driveway. By the time I'm inside I've forgotten the entire evening.

Stewart will be home in four days.

The night Stewart is released from Spring Meadow, I go for a long walk around my neighborhood. I picture Stewart waiting at the Carlton Greyhound station. I imagine him getting on the bus, settling into a seat, watching out the window, the long ride to his mom's house in Centralia.

I walk down our street, past the little playground by the park. I think about other boys I've liked over the years. Craig Lessing, from fourth grade. Ryan Jones, in junior high, who used to sell pot behind the bowling alley. Rex Hemple, the guy I lost my virginity to in a nearby field after we drank a fifth of his father's best whiskey.

I remember that night especially, stumbling up the street, still drunk, my clothes askew, my body not quite my own. And other nights from the Mad Dog era: getting dropped off by older boys in cars full of throbbing beats and dope smoke. Or being dumped at the bottom of the hill by pissed-off girlfriends. Or being released into my parents' custody by the always helpful officers of the West Linn Police Department.

Tonight, though, the neighborhood is perfectly calm, perfectly quiet. I can clear my mind of everything but the image of Stewart and our future together. Whatever happens, he will always be the first boy I truly gave my heart to. Which makes him a caretaker, a holder of something. He holds me. I am his in a way he probably isn't even aware of.

And a good thing too. Boys shouldn't know what power they have. They would panic probably, or just mess things up. But boys are who you give yourself to. Not your parents, or your teachers, or your "future." You give yourself to a boy.

And then you go for long walks at night and think about them and wonder what they will do to you in the end.

12

Friday is the day.

I wake up early, take a long shower, dress carefully in an outfit I have been planning for weeks.

I go to school. I go to my morning classes. At lunch, I sit in the library and eat my carrots.

I go to my afternoon classes. The teachers teach. The students listen. I hear nothing, see nothing.

When school gets out, I walk the three blocks to the MAX train station and ride it downtown. I walk to the big Central Library where I'm meeting Stewart at five.

I'm wearing my favorite skirt, leggings, a cinched vintage raincoat, sunglasses. I remain in a trance until I see the actual library. That's when my heart starts to race, my palms begin to sweat. But I must remain calm. No schoolgirl-crush behavior. I have to be worthy of Stewart.

I walk up the stone steps and sit on the bench outside. Though it is still February, there is a hint of spring in the air. Birds chirp in the trees. A row of purple flowers are trying to bloom along the sides of the building.

Library-type people walk up the stone steps. I watch a college girl getting signatures for Greenpeace. A man with a briefcase strides up the steps with purpose.

For a moment, I have trouble imagining Stewart in this scene. It's hard to imagine him in any part of normal life. He's too cool, too larger than life.

But then he appears. He comes striding down the street and I am shocked — like I always seem to be — by how young and carefree and innocent he appears.

Whatever plan I had, whatever dignified welcome-home speech I had prepared, is completely forgotten once he's in sight. I leap up and run toward him. He sees me and his face lights up. I race down the steps and throw myself into his arms, as onlookers make way, grinning to themselves.

"Hey, you," he says, lifting me off my feet.

I cannot speak. *Stewart, my love, my Lost Prince.* I hug him so long and hard my arms start to hurt. And even then, I stay like that for as long as he'll let me.

13

We head toward the center of town. The sun is coming out a little. I smile at people on the street. I am so happy.

We stop at a Starbucks and I order us both hot chocolates, even though I think Stewart wants a normal coffee.

"Tough," I tell him. "You're having hot chocolate and I'm buying."

Stewart grumbles and finds us a table. He's being his awkward, adorable self. A foursome of high school girls totally stop talking to gawk at how gorgeous he is.

I ignore this. I bring the hot chocolate and give him his and sit.

For a moment we don't speak. We just grin at each other.

"So what's it like, out here in the real world?" he asks me finally.

"It sucks," I say. "But it just got a whole lot better."

He smiles into his cup.

We talk about stuff. His living situation. The weirdness of high school. I tell him about Trish and our day at the hospital.

At one point, he looks at my finger. He sees the ring. I see that he sees it and I smile bashfully.

I don't say anything, though.

After Starbucks, we walk around downtown. We watch some kids skateboarding. We eat some Chinese spring rolls from a trailer. We sit on a park bench and I lean against him, holding his arm, doing nothing, basically, just getting to know each other again.

When it gets dark, Stewart suggests we go to a movie. I feel like our time is too precious for that, but if that's what he wants . . .

It'll be like movie night, I think.

We go inside and get tickets. This is a real theater, though. It costs twelve bucks a ticket. Popcorn costs six dollars. I pay.

We sit and watch the previews. I cuddle up next to Stewart as best as I can, but it's hard because the seats are stiff and plastic and there's cup holders in the way and headrests on the seats in front of you so you can't put your feet up.

"I haven't been to a movie since I went with you," I tell Stewart.

"Yeah?" he says.

"This guy wanted to go, but I wouldn't."

"Huh."

"He was just a friend. Not a guy guy. Just this boy from school who I got stuck with one night."

Stewart doesn't say anything. I shouldn't have mentioned it. That was stupid.

The movie starts. I barely watch it. I just try to snuggle up with Stewart as much as I can. I take deep sniffs of him, I can't really help it.

He pats me on the head like I'm a love-starved puppy. Which is pretty much what I am.

. . .

When we leave the theater, the streets are quiet and the air is cold and still. I slip my hand around Stewart's elbow. I want to walk him back to the bus station, but since it's ten o'clock, he wants to put me on the MAX train and get me home to my parents.

"You're in high school," he says, teasing me. "You have homework."

I let him walk me to the MAX station and the minute we get there, the train comes. I refuse to leave until he gives me a real kiss good-bye, so he does and it's heavenly. But it's weird too, in some way. I don't know how to describe it. There's a reserve on his end. Like he's scared of me, or he thinks I'm too young. I can't tell what it is.

The love-starved puppy thing. Maybe he doesn't like that. Or the fact that I've paid for everything.

When the next train pulls up, it's 10:30 and he insists I go. I refuse. So he picks me up and carries me onto it. He puts me down in a seat and then dashes out just as the doors are closing. I immediately run to the window and press my forehead against the glass and stare at him.

I still have his ring. I point at it, through the glass.

He grins and gestures not to worry. I blow him a kiss. He waves good-bye.

The train starts to move and I stare at him, watching him as long as I can. Then he is gone and I collapse in my seat.

I feel so happy I can barely stand it. I feel so happy I want to get high. For half a second I wonder if Jeff Weed is still downtown. Could I call Jake? Or Raj?

But then I remember who I am, what I am, what my situation is.

No, I tell myself. *I cannot.*

14

The next day at lunch, Martin Farris is waiting for me in the library for some reason. He is sitting at our usual table.

Martin's got a big Taco Bell bag in front of him.

"What's that?"

"That's our lunch," he says. "I have an idea."

"What's your idea?"

"That you come eat this with me in the cafeteria."

"Why would I do that?"

"Because you can't hide in the library every lunch period for the rest of your life."

I look at him. "Don't do this, Martin."

"What?" he says. "You think it's a good idea to never go into the cafeteria again?"

"It's none of your business. Who cares if I go or not?"

"I do," he says confidently. "It bugs me that you won't eat in the cafeteria. It's not right."

"It's not your problem," I say.

"Who are you so afraid of that you can't go in there?"

I glance up at him for a moment. "Trust me, there's nobody in this high school that I'm afraid of."

"Then why won't you eat where everyone else eats?"

I have no response to these arguments and so, to shut him up, I follow him into the cafeteria.

When we first walk in I see immediately that I was right to avoid this place. It is loud and awful and full of shrieking children. We walk by a table that includes Emily Brantley and some of her crew. She sees me and says something and immediately all her friends start laughing.

Thanks, Martin.

Oh yeah, and another thing. I'm with *Martin Farris*. That helps a lot. To finally show my face in public with one of the biggest geeks in the school. This is *such* a great idea.

But then we sit and nothing particularly bad happens. Martin patiently opens the Taco Bell bag. He hands me a burrito. He takes one himself. He opens his and takes a bite. "Eat," he commands.

I'm still sort of looking around at the other people. But I do as I'm told. I take a bite. The burrito is pretty good. I take another bite. The weird panic in my chest settles down. And nobody really notices me anyway because I've barely even gone to this school if you think about it. The worst of "Mad Dog Maddie" was over a year ago. Nobody remembers. Nobody cares.

And then I find myself watching the other students: infant-sized freshmen, an artistic-looking girl with round glasses, a little gang of long-haired sophomore skater boys who are totally cute.

So as people-watching goes, it's okay. Not the greatest. But not the worst either.

15

After school, Emily Brantley catches me in the parking lot. I'm calling my mom to pick me up and Emily swings in front of me in her black Saab.

"Hey, Rehab Girl, wanna ride?" she calls out. She's wearing a Hurley baseball cap that once belonged to Raj.

"No, thanks. My mom is coming."

"Call her back," she says. "Tell her you got a ride. I need to ask you something."

I don't know what Emily wants with me. But I'm a little curious to find out. Also, my mom has a cooking class and won't be here for a half hour.

I get in the car with Emily. She takes off, flying over the speed bumps and then rocketing out of the parking lot. "Wanna get a slice of pizza?" she says.

"Not really," I say, hanging on for dear life.

"I do. Do you mind?"

"I guess not."

We bounce into the parking lot of Hot Lips Pizza down the street. There are other people from Evergreen there. Emily Brantley is notorious at our high school for partying, for being hot, and for hooking up with people. So the other kids take notice when we walk in.

Emily gets a slice of pepperoni and we sit in the prized corner booth that miraculously opens up as soon as we need it.

Emily slides in and takes a big bite of her pizza.

"So," she says.

"So what?" I ask, sitting there, watching her.

"How are you doing?"

"I'm doing fine, Emily. Is that all you wanted to know?"

"No, actually. Why are you being so touchy?"

"Maybe because you and your friends were laughing at me today in the cafeteria?"

"What are you talking about? We weren't laughing at you. Don't be so paranoid."

It occurs to me that I'm not actually sure they were laughing at me.

"I wanted to ask you something," says Emily. "About my sister."

"I didn't know you had a sister."

"I do. She's a freshman. And she's having problems."

I wasn't expecting this. "I'm hardly the person to talk to about that," I say, watching a gang of Evergreen boys huddled around an arcade game.

"It's not school problems she's having. It's party problems. She's a party girl. And not in a good way. She got so drunk last weekend she passed out in Raleigh Park. The police found her."

That's weird. The first time I ever got really drunk, I passed out in Raleigh Park. And the police found me.

"My parents are freaking out. Obviously. Other people are like, she's fine, she just doesn't know how to drink. But she *does* know how to drink. That's what's so scary. She could drink you or me under the table."

I doubt that, but I say nothing.

"She hangs out with Bryce Handler. That's another problem. She's totally hot. She gets whatever she wants. Especially from guys."

"What's her name?"

"Ashley. I doubt you know her. She's making a name for herself, though. That's for sure." Emily leans a little closer. "People think I'm bad? She's like me *times ten*."

"That's a lot," I say.

Emily takes a bite of her pizza. "I just thought you might have some advice."

"You could send her to rehab," I offer. "There was a girl at my place who was fifteen."

"I think my parents want to send her to one of those boot camp things. Tough love, or whatever. Are those better, do you think?"

"I have no idea," I say. "None of it works, unless the person wants to change."

"That's what I was trying to tell my mother. Ashley isn't exactly at that stage. The thing about her is, she'll do whatever will piss the most people off. She's kind of a drama person."

"Aren't we all," I say. "Aren't we all."

16

I haven't heard from Trish since the hospital, and then she calls. She just wants to say hi, see how I'm doing. I'm fine, I tell her. She scared me pretty good at the hospital, but I have to admit, it's a relief to hear her voice.

We talk about random things. She's been looking for guys online. She meets them in coffee shops. She tried to sign up for eHarmony but they rejected her because of her lack of Christian values "and basically because I'm a total whore," she tells me.

She makes it all into a big joke, how pathetic she is, how nobody wants her, except bald forty-year-old guys who are married. . . .

She doesn't sound good.

So I agree to go shopping with her, and on Friday we go to Nordstrom downtown. This doesn't make me feel any better about her mental state. She buys these bizarre shoes that cost too much and then buys a bunch of cheesy lingerie. Then, as we're leaving, she can't find her wallet, which is no surprise, since she's totally crazed when she's shopping and pays no attention to anything.

We have to go back to the counter where she paid, but the saleslady doesn't have it. So then we go into the dressing room to see if it fell out there but we can't find it. So then we report it to the manager and make a big scene and it becomes this big search for the missing wallet. The whole Nordstrom staff is looking for it and then Trish suddenly gets all panicked and I have to hustle her away.

We go to Metro Café, and I get us tea and we sit at the big table in the back. I try to calm her down by going through all the crap she bought. That's when I find her wallet in the bottom of one of her shopping bags. I throw it onto the table in front of her and she starts laughing like a crazy person.

All of which freaks me out. And the really scary thing is: She's still pretty much my best friend.

What that says about me, I do not know.

Meanwhile, I'm constantly trying to figure out ways to see Stewart. Which isn't easy, since he lives in Centralia, which is impossible to get to.

We finally work something out for the next weekend. His mom is heading off to Las Vegas, so I will go to him.

I feel like it's pretty clear what's going to happen when we're alone in his house together. I hope that's what will happen, anyway. On the other hand, I've never been with a boy sober. So, who knows?

On Saturday morning, I take the MAX downtown, and then get on the Greyhound to Centralia. Stewart is waiting for me there, in an old truck that barely runs and doesn't have license plates or insurance.

The truck almost dies, but we make it back to his mom's house.

Stewart is in a good mood, but he still doesn't say much. It feels weird to have to plan something like this. As we drive, it seems odd that we talk so little. I feel like I have slipped somehow in his mind. That I've faded slightly. We're not the same couple that walked home in the rain from the Exxon station that night.

On the other hand, if today doesn't get me back in his mind, I don't know what will.

We get to his mom's, which is a small box of a house, with an unkempt lawn, at the end of a gravel road. The other houses are kind of run-down as well. It's not the best neighborhood.

Stewart goes quiet when he shuts off the truck. We walk up the gravel driveway. But then, the minute we get inside, Stewart starts kissing me. I'm surprised he's this direct. I wasn't expecting it. He peels off his shirt and takes off mine. He undoes his belt. I can't really read his face. I can't tell what he's thinking.

I don't let him take off the rest of my clothes. I get in the bed and for a minute my mouth goes dry and I don't know if I even want to do this.

He feels weird too. I can tell. He leaves the room, comes back with a can of Coke, which he opens and drinks, sitting on the side of the bed.

I lie there with the covers up to my neck, staring at his long, smooth back.

"You okay?" I ask him.

"Are you?"

"I'm sort of nervous," I say.

"Me too." He drinks from his Coke. "Sorry to jump you like that."

"It's okay."

He stares down at the Coke can. I see it then: *He's worried he's not good enough for me.*

"Stewart," I say quietly.

"Yeah."

"I love you."

"You sure?"

"Yes."

He turns and smiles. "Okay, then."

The sex is weird. How could it not be? And the fact that it's in broad daylight doesn't help. We fumble with our clothes. I can't get my bra off. Stewart gets tangled in his pants and nearly falls off the bed.

When everything is ready we're both so nervous, we just sort of stop. His skin — which always feels so warm and soft — suddenly feels cold to the touch, and I can tell when he kisses me that he is unsure, and so am I, and nothing we do seems to work. Only when we give up and start laughing about what a disaster this is, do we actually relax and gradually find each other in a real way.

But from that moment on, it's perfect. Coming together, unrushed, unquestioning, with no hesitation and no regret. And it does feel amazing and we watch each other and stare into each other's eyes.

When it's over I curl up inside his thick arms, and drift off into a dreamless sleep.

18

When I wake up, it's dark. Stewart is in the kitchen. I can see him through the door, in his boxers, lighting the stove and looking around for a pan. He asks me if I want scrambled eggs. He's got the radio on and turns up "Sweet Emotion" when it plays.

I gather the comforter around my naked shoulders and go into the kitchen. I sit at the table. I remain silent, smiling, watching Stewart do a master chef impersonation. He's dashing around. Putting cheese on the eggs. Making toast. Pretending to speak French. He's having a great time.

Then, while the eggs spatter, he comes to me — the spatula still in one hand — bends over, holds my face, and kisses my forehead.

"If you could see how adorable you look right now," he says to me.

I smile happily and he kisses me again on the top of the head.

"You know what I've been thinkin'?" he says to me.

"What's that?"

"I'm gonna dye my hair black."

"Yeah?"

"This girl . . . from down the street. She's a hairdresser. She said she'd do me for free if I wanted."

I nod. "But blondes have more fun," I say.

"They do, don't they?" he says, grinning back toward me.

I smile at him. Then I pull the old comforter closer around my shoulders.

The girl down the street, I think. *She'll do me for free.*

But no, I can't get like that. I can't be jealous. I won't be.

Stewart risks getting pulled over and drives me all the way back to the MAX train afterward in his broken-down pickup. We talk off and on. He manages to never mention that we just slept together. Or what that might mean. Instead he tells me about fixing motorcycles with a guy who has a little garage outside Centralia. It might turn into an actual job.

Then he sees me playing with his grandmother's ring.

"The ring!" he says. "You still have it!"

"Of course I still have it," I say. "What did you think?"

"And you're wearing it. That's so awesome."

"Just until you got back. Do you want it?"

"No way. You keep it. That way I know it's safe."

"You gotta take it back at some point. It's yours."

"It's both of ours now. Don't you think?"

"No. It's your grandmother's," I say, turning it around on my finger. "I'm just holding it for you."

He grins at me then. "I can't think of a better place for it."

"Really?" I say.

"Totally," he says.

And for a moment, everything seems perfect again.

part three

My dad continues his adventures in the solar energy business. This actually affects my life. Many times I come home and there are important people at the house, foreign investors, local politicians, rich people who are trying to get richer. Always I am introduced and always I shake hands and conduct myself with the utmost dignity.

Caterers appear regularly in our driveway. They smoke sometimes, in secret, behind the bushes by our mailbox. A real espresso machine (from Italy) is installed in our kitchen. That's probably my favorite thing. The cocktail parties are my least favorite. I don't like the smell of alcohol wafting up from the living room. Or the strange, half-drunk grown-ups wandering the halls outside my bedroom.

My father's schedule is unpredictable. One week he's home in his study working twelve hours a day. The next week he's off to the East Coast or Japan doing God knows what. My mom and I, when left alone, tend to retreat to different ends of the house. I am grateful for these stretches of solitude. I can catch up on my TiVo watching.

• • •

Then, on Tuesday of spring break, we suddenly pack up and fly to Aspen, Colorado, for an emergency work meeting for my dad. My mother is very excited about this. I am too, though I have no idea what I'm going to do with myself in such a place.

It's a three-hour flight. I sit with my book bag under the seat and a copy of *Lord of the Flies* in my lap. I think I'm going to read but what I mostly do is think about Stewart. I imagine he's sitting with me, we're talking, joking around, holding hands on the armrest. I talk to him in my head, explaining things, my family, how my dad is a workaholic and my mother can't deal with it, withdraws, and then gets mad at me for no reason.

Or — and this is best of all — I think about the day at his mom's house: the way his back looked in the afternoon light, the touch of his fingertips, the tiny whisker stubs around his lips and cheeks and sideburns. How strange it was to be so close to someone. And how amazing.

It's a nice place to be, warm and fuzzy inside my thoughts, replaying certain moments . . . until my parents interrupt me . . . or the flight attendant . . . or we have to put on our seat belts for the landing. . . .

2

One thing about staying in a nice hotel is that you can forget you're a dorky high school kid.

The first night in Aspen I spend sitting in the lobby watching people and pretending to read *Lord of the Flies*. I order a cup of Earl Grey tea from the bar. It all feels very grown up . . . until a suave young man in a tuxedo comes over and asks me where the ballroom is and I blurt out: "I don't know, I'm in high school!"

The next morning, I try to make up for this by putting on my biggest sunglasses and my vintage raincoat (cinched) and going for a very sophisticated walk around my hotel. This is really fun because boys check me out and older dudes too, and nobody really knows what my deal is. And later, sitting in a famous Aspen café, drinking an espresso with a lemon twist and reading *Vogue*, I call Trish and play the "Guess where I am right now" game, which is great fun because she really plays it:

"Are you glamorous or ridiculous?"

"Glamorous."

"Vintage or twenty-first century?"

"Mostly vintage."

"East Coast or West Coast?"

"In the middle, sort of."

"Are there celebrities present?"

"There are pictures of celebrities on the walls. Signed."

This conversation makes me miss her and reminds me she is the only girlfriend I have who really gets me at this point in my life.

The following night, my dad gets invited to a fancy dinner party and I have to come too since the people have kids in high school.

We drive our rental SUV to a cabin that's far out in the woods. I get introduced to the various sons and daughters of people who are there.

So then I have to hang out. That's not as easy as it sounds. Amy Smithline, who I end up sitting next to at dinner, goes on and on about being accepted to Columbia University in New York City. "It's Ivy League, you know," she tells me about three times. "People forget that it's Ivy League because it's in Manhattan. But I think it's the best of both worlds. I wouldn't even want to go to Yale. Have you ever seen New Haven? It's a dump!"

After dinner I escape and go sit next to two boys by the fireplace named Peter and Chad. They're smartly avoiding the Amy Smithline situation by roasting marshmallows. We talk a little. I mostly watch them eat.

Then they ask me if I want to come walk the dog with them. At first I hesitate, but then my mom helpfully orders me to go, claiming that it'll be fun, that I need to get out and enjoy the mountain air.

So I go. We put on our coats in the hallway. Peter and Chad are both good-looking in a classical preppy kind of way. They have expensive parkas, L.L.Bean snow boots, Norwegian ski hats.

They get the dog and we take it outside. We walk a few yards down the driveway and Chad immediately pulls a joint out of his coat pocket and lights it.

I don't say anything. They kinda had a stoner vibe about them, so I'm not really surprised.

Chad takes a big hit and gives it to Peter. Peter takes a hit and offers it to me.

"No, thanks," I say, bending down to pet the dog.

"You don't smoke weed?" he asks, surprised.

"Nah."

"Why not?"

"It sorta . . . gives me a headache," I lie.

"It relieves my headache!" jokes Chad.

Peter takes another hit.

The weed smoke smells *good*. My head spins for a minute and I know I have to move away. I let the dog lead me down the driveway a little ways. I find a stick and throw it into the woods. I follow the dog until I'm out of sight of the boys.

Because it's so quiet, I can still hear Chad and Peter whispering on the driveway:

"I hate chicks who won't party," says Chad, taking a hit off the joint.

"Too bad. She was cute too," says Peter.

"Gives me a headache?" says Chad. "You're just an uptight bitch, why don't you just admit it."

I find the stick and throw it for the dog. He runs deeper into the woods. I run deeper too.

A few minutes later, Chad calls out: "Hey, whatever your name was! Bring the dog in when you're done! We're going back inside!"

"Okay!" I yell back.

When they're gone, I lie down on my back in the snow and sigh with deep relief.

Then the dog comes bounding through the snow. He jumps on my chest and licks my face.

3

Back at our hotel, I sit on a couch in the lobby and call Stewart's mom's house. He actually answers for a change, but he can't talk. He and his friend are out in the garage taking apart someone's Harley-Davidson. "You can't really stop in the middle," he tells me.

I don't let him off that easy, though. I want to know when we can hang out again.

That's when he tells me about his plan to go find his dad. "My sister just talked to him. He's down in Redland," he tells me. Redland is a famous pot-farm hippie town in southern Oregon.

"What's he doing down there?" I ask.

"Nobody knows. Nobody's talked to him in four years. The thing is, I can't deal with my mom anymore. She's been hitting me up for money and stuff."

"That's not good."

"I gotta find my dad. I gotta find one person in my family who's halfway sane."

"But what about your sister?"

"She's okay. But her boyfriend's into some bad business too."

I have no answer to that. "How long will you be gone for?"
I ask.

"I don't know. I haven't talked to him yet."

I don't know how to respond. The phone on his side goes
silent too.

"Did you dye your hair black?" I ask.

"Not yet."

"You know I like the blond. I mean, I like it either way."

"Yeah, I like the blond too. I dunno."

"I miss you so much," I tell him.

"I miss you too."

"I wish I could be with you tonight."

"Me too."

"I think about you all the time."

"Yeah."

"I love you," I say.

There's a pause. And then he says it. "I love you too,
Maddie."

But then I can't think of where to go from there. Maybe
that's enough. It should be enough.

But somehow it isn't.

4

On my last day in Aspen, I take a snowboarding lesson and then sit around in the lodge, looking glamorous. At one point I see Chad and Peter. They come running over like I'm their best friend, but I tell them some excuse and escape.

When we get home from Aspen on Sunday, we're all pretty fried. I unpack my stuff, dump my laundry down the laundry chute, dump my schoolwork on the floor. Naturally, I still haven't finished *Lord of the Flies*.

My parents are downstairs, but then my mother comes up and knocks on my bedroom door.

"Maddie?" she says in an odd tone. "There's a voice-mail message for you."

I try to think who it could be. Not Stewart, he would call my phone.

"I think it's important," says my mother.

I put my bathrobe on and open the door. My mother has a very strange expression on her face. I go downstairs, where my father is standing in the dining room doorway. His face is ashen gray.

"Jeez, you guys," I say to both of them, picking up the phone. "Did somebody die?"

My mother turns away. I put the phone to my ear. To my surprise it is an adult voice.

It's Trish's mother. Somebody did die. Trish died.

5

t was a guy. Of course it was.

It was a twenty-eight-year-old convicted felon named Mark Hastings. He and two friends were on the MAX train on Friday night, on their way to score drugs. That's when they met Trish, who was coming home from her job at Don's Carpet Warehouse.

I can picture the scene: Trish on the train, coming home from her boring job, heading back to her boring house. A cute guy appears as if by magic. He's confident, cool, totally unlike the parade of losers she's met online. He smooth-talks her a little, charms her. She gets all gushy like she does. And of course she'll do anything he wants. She'll go anywhere. Even help him buy drugs if that's what it takes.

According to the police report, Trish went with Hastings and his friends to North Portland, where they bought about five hundred dollars worth of cocaine and heroin. Trish willingly contributed eighty dollars of her own money to this purchase. Obviously she really liked Mark Hastings.

An hour later, they checked into the nearby Saturn Hotel. The heat in the room was turned up full blast. Beers were passed around. Hastings and the others stripped to their underwear and danced to loud music (there were complaints). They began to take the drugs they had bought.

At around 1:00 a.m., Trish, who was sitting on a bed with Hastings, became so intoxicated she became sick. She attempted to crawl over Hastings, to get to the bathroom ("probably to throw up," one of the medical examiners wrote). In the process, she fell off the bed, landed on her face, and broke her nose. It was then that she lost consciousness and perhaps suffered cardiac arrest.

She was not discovered by Hastings until several hours later, when he tripped over her leg. He tried to talk to her and realized she had stopped breathing.

Hastings and the others dragged her into the shower and turned cold water on her. This did not revive her. They then attempted CPR, which none of them knew how to perform properly.

When she didn't respond, Hastings and the others fled the scene. They later claimed they called 911, but no such call was recorded. They most likely feared a murder charge. So they did nothing. They went home, where they were later found and arrested.

The following afternoon, a hotel maid discovered Trish. According to the maid's statement, Trish was a greenish white color, she was nearly naked, there was dried blood and vomit around her mouth and nose. The maid called an ambulance, and Patricia Carrie Morgan was pronounced dead on the scene at 2:12 p.m.

'm standing in my backyard with my phone.

"But you have to come, Stewart! I need you."

"But I already made the arrangements," he tells me. "My dad is expecting me."

"Tell him something came up!"

"I can't wait a week. My mom thinks I'm leaving. Her boyfriend is living here already."

"But what about *me*?"

"I'm sorry. I would totally stay. But there's nothing I can do."

I can't believe this. I have just spent an afternoon at Trish's house, talking to the police, dealing with her devastated parents, calming down her little sister.

"Can you at least come over? Can I see you?" I ask Stewart.

"When?"

"Anytime. Now. Tonight."

"I'm taking a bunch of stuff over to my sister's. And she needs her car."

"Can you come afterward?"

"How am I going to get there?"

"Take the bus! Stewart, *my best friend just died.*"

"Okay," he says, taking a deep breath. "I'll come."

The only place I can meet Stewart is the downtown bus station. My parents don't like the sound of that. My mom says she'll drive me there, and come pick me up. But I tell her no, I'll take the MAX.

"Take the car, then," she says.

"How can I?" I say. "I have no insurance."

She tells me I do have insurance. They renewed it for me, as of spring break, since I was doing so well and even though my insurance rate is astronomical.

This is a surprise. "Are you serious?" I say to her.

She is. My dad nods too. They both are.

So now I have a car, the Volvo station wagon no less. This, at least, is good news.

But I don't have much time. I drive downtown and wait for Stewart at the bus station.

When he comes out, I hug him for a long time. Then I bring him back to my car.

"What's this?" he asks when he sees the Volvo.

"It's my parents'."

"Nice," he says, getting in. He starts fiddling with the dials. "Are these seat warmers?"

"My parents have money," I tell him in a low voice. I'm starting to get pissed. No, I was already pissed. Now I'm more pissed.

I drive us to Denny's. We sit in a booth. I have some things I want to say to Stewart. But once we're there, none of them seem important. Once we're sitting there, all I can think about is Trish, and I start crying. I can't help it. Stewart reaches over and takes my hand. But this is too much for him. I can see it in his face. He can't process it. He doesn't know how to be there for someone.

"I'm really sorry," he says later as we sit in the Volvo in the parking lot. "I know I'm not handling this right." Then he takes me in his arms and holds me for a long time while I cry. He kisses my forehead. He strokes my hair.

This is better. This is what I wanted all along. We kiss a little and then go back to holding each other.

"I just want you to be okay," he whispers.

After that, I wish I could stay with him all night. I wish that I lived with him, that we were married, that we could be together forever.

That's how it is with Stewart. It always ends up that I love him no matter what.

The funeral isn't until Saturday, and I still have the rest of the week to deal with.

On Wednesday, after lunch, I'm standing at my locker and I sense someone behind me. I turn around and there are two freshman girls standing there. One of them is really cute. Shockingly cute. And dressed like she knows it.

As I turn, they kind of shuffle away. I don't know who they are, or what they want. They get a little way down the hall and the really cute one turns back toward me. Our eyes meet. She has this strange expression on her face. A sort of arrogance, or superiority, like she owns these hallways. So why is she bothering me?

But then I realize who it is. It's Ashley Brantley. Emily Brantley's party-girl sister.

What does *she* want?

Thursday after school, I drive to Centralia, to say good-bye to Stewart before he leaves for Redland.

He answers the door, shirtless, drinking a Red Bull. His hair is freshly dyed black. It shines. He's very proud of it.

He wants me to touch it. I do. I stroke it. Then he grabs me and he picks me up and carries me inside, though I'm not really in that sort of mood.

It's nice to be here, though. It's nice to forget about my own life for a second and be part of Stewart's carefree world.

Later, I drive him down to Rite Aid, so he can get some stuff for his trip. We goof around in the Rite Aid. I remember waiting for him at the Rite Aid in Carlton. I ask him if he remembers.

"That was quite a night," he says in not quite the right tone.

Later, though, when I'm leaving, he becomes more serious. We stand together in the driveway, leaning against my car. He tells me more stuff he's learned about his father in Redland. He's got a little business building decks and installing hot tubs. He lives in a little cabin in the mountains he built himself.

"He sounded great," Stewart tells me. "I can't wait to see him."

I nod my encouragement. I'm genuinely happy for him.

"So when will you get back?" I ask.

"Not sure."

"But I mean, like, three days, or a week, or what?"

"I don't know," he says again. "I don't think I can stay with my mom anymore."

"You can't live in Redland."

"Maybe I can," he says quietly. "For a little while anyway."

I'm surprised by this. I didn't know this was an option. "But what then?"

"I don't know. I'll just have to see."

"You mean you'd move down there? Permanently?"

"I gotta live somewhere."

I stare at him. "What's wrong with here? You don't have to live with your mother. Get your own place."

"With what money?"

"I don't know. Get a job."

He shuffles his feet. "Listen to you. You sound like someone's wife."

I stare at him. "So how long were you thinking, then?"

"He said I could maybe work for him. In that case it would be for the summer."

"The *summer*?" I say. "You'd stay down there all *summer*?!"

"Well, yeah . . ."

"Do you even *want* to be with me?"

"Don't say that," he says, frustrated. "Of course I do. Maybe not exactly the way you want."

"What does that mean?"

He turns sideways to me. "I just think you want a lot. You want me to call you all the time. You want me to get a job. You want me to be like somebody's high school boyfriend or something."

"When did I ever say that?"

"But of course you do. That's what every girl wants."

"I *never* said that. I never said anything like that. All I ever wanted was for us to be together. And then let things work out . . . however they were meant to."

"I know," says Stewart. "That's what I want too."

I turn toward my mom's car. Tears are coming to my eyes. It's starting to sink in, what this conversation means.

"You said you loved me," I say quietly.

"I do love you," mumbles Stewart. "That's not the issue."

More tears are coming. *I'm losing Stewart,* I think. Right here and now. I can't believe it's happening. I've lost Trish. And now I'm losing Stewart.

I dab my eyes. When I turn back, Stewart is still standing

there. He looks miserable. But he also looks determined. Like he's doing what he's doing and that's it.

It's gotten late. I have to get home. I take off his grandmother's ring. I step forward and hold it out.

"What are you doing?" he asks me.

"I'm giving you your ring back."

"What? No. That's yours!"

"No, it's not," I say. "It's yours. It's your grandmother's. And if you're gonna be in Redland all summer, you're gonna need it more than I will."

"Seriously," he says. "I gave you that. I want you to have it. I want to know it's with you."

"I'm not keeping it," I say. I walk up to his front step and leave it on the railing.

I go to my car. I open the door.

"Wait!" he says. He grabs me. He tries to say something, but he can't find the words.

I see the frustration in his face and it occurs to me that I've been unfair. I've asked him to be something he's not. I want him to do things he isn't capable of yet.

He's just Stewart. Goofy, adorable, messed-up Stewart. Why am I being so hard on him?

I grab him. I hug him. I kiss him.

But I leave the ring. Because he's the one who'll need it now.

8

Martin comes with me to Trish's funeral. I pick him up at his house. I somehow get talked into coming inside and meeting his parents. I don't know how this happens. They're perfectly nice and all. But this isn't a date.

We drive to the cemetery. Martin wears a suit and a tie. I'm wearing a navy blue dress and my mother's black cardigan.

When we get to the cemetery, I'm not sure where the funeral is. I assume we'll find it by the crowd of people.

I'm also assuming Cynthia, our counselor, will be there. I expect a bunch of staff people from Spring Meadow to show up. Angela, maybe, and some of the other women we lived with.

I imagine Haley might be there — despite everything — in her wheelchair, with her nurse and her family. And some of Trish's other friends from high school. And of course all the cousins or relatives or whatever.

But I'm wrong about the crowd. I realize this slowly, as I drive in circles around the cemetery. Finally I spot the Cadillac Escalade, parked with two other cars under a tree.

I pull over. Martin and I stare across the lawn at the seven people standing at the grave.

"Is that it?" says Martin.

Oh no, I think to myself.

But there's nothing to be done. We have to go. We lock the car and walk through the wet grass.

The people present are her dad, her mom, her sister, an older woman, and two men from the funeral home. Martin and I are the only people close to Trish's age.

The truth comes to me then. *I was her only friend.*

We stand at the grave site. I look across at her mother, who sees nothing, hears nothing, is utterly lost in grief.

The group of us stand and wait. A priest is coming. I can see him walking slowly through the grass.

Martin coughs into his fist. He's acting very formal. He keeps his chin up, his hands joined in front of him. It's an odd posture.

"You don't have to do that," I whisper to him.

"Do what?"

"Stand funny," I say.

"I'm not standing funny."

The priest finally arrives. He gets out his Bible. He reads something no one listens to.

Martin is still standing weird.

"Stop doing that," I whisper to him.

"Doing what?" he whispers back, annoyed.

The priest says a few words about Trish. It's obvious he knows nothing about her. When he's finished there's a quiet moment of prayer.

They begin to lower the casket into the ground.

Her mom lets out an unearthly wail. She makes an awkward lunge toward the casket, falling to her knees in the muddy grass and crawling toward the hole. The men jump forward and grab her up by the armpits. They drag her back. The sister stares blankly forward.

"Good-bye, Trish," I blurt without meaning to.

Trish's little sister looks up when I say this. But when she sees me, her face registers nothing.

Martin coughs into his fist. I watch the casket disappear into the black earth.

They always say you go to a better place when you die. That you are finally at peace. I never believed that before. But in Trish's case, it might be true.

She had no place on this earth. There was no place where she was comfortable, no place she could relax, no place where she felt safe.

I never saw her happy. I never saw her at ease. Not for one moment.

Good-bye, Trish.

When I get home, my parents wait to see how I'm holding up. I tell them I'm okay. I just want to go upstairs to my room. I want to take a bath.

That night, I sit at my desk. I turn my radio on. I have nothing to do really. Stewart is in Redland. Trish is gone.

I do have homework. I have a lot of that. Maybe I should do some.

I open my book bag and look inside. I have an American history quiz on Monday. I was gonna do my usual: skim the chapters in study hall and get my C.

But now I get the book out and open to the first of the assigned chapters. I turn the radio down and turn on my overhead light.

I smooth the page. What would happen if I read the whole chapter? If I actually *studied* it?

I try it. I start reading. I find that I have good concentration. My brain seems relieved to have something neutral to think about.

I read each sentence carefully, making sure I understand it. Then I go to the next sentence, to the next paragraph.

I get through the whole chapter. I get out a notebook and write down the main points. It's not really that hard, if you actually focus.

Then I turn to the next chapter. I read that. On the last page, they tell you the three things they want you to remember. I write those down. I say them over again, touching my pen to each point and thinking about them until I understand why they're important.

I continue forward through the next chapter, writing other things down, taking careful notes.

I continue like this for nearly two hours, which is a record for me. When I finally turn off my desk light, I am drained. But I also feel strangely satisfied, not to mention proud of myself.

On Monday, I take the test. I get a one hundred.

Usually Martin sits with me at lunch. The Monday after the funeral he doesn't come to the cafeteria. I look for him at his locker, but he's not there either.

Then I see him in the breezeway hanging with some of his nerd buddies.

I try to join in, but they ignore me. I try to get Martin's attention. He ignores me too.

I tug on his sleeve. "Hey," I say.

He doesn't answer. His nerd buddies are talking about superhero movies. Could Iron Man take Batman in a fight? Stuff like that.

"Uh, hello? Martin?" I say again, quietly so his friends don't hear. "Care to tell me what's going on?"

"What?" he snaps.

I step back. "What's the matter?" I ask.

"What do you think?"

"I . . . I don't know," I say. "Are you mad at me?"

He stomps off, away from his friends. I follow. He won't talk to me, though. He keeps walking. He's actually mad at me. Martin Farris is *pissed*.

"Martin?" I say, very serious now. "What is it? What did I do?"

"What *don't* you do?" he says bitterly.

"Martin? You have to tell me what it is."

"I just wish we could do one thing together where you didn't have to tell me what a dork I am. That's it. That's all. Just *one thing*."

I walk along behind him. "When did I call you a dork?"

He stops, turns on me: "You do it constantly. You're *always* criticizing me. Like at the funeral. Telling me how to stand. I mean, seriously. Do you think how I *stand* has anything to do with you?"

"How you stand? What are you talking about?"

"The funeral. I go to the funeral. I wear my little coat and tie. I try to conduct myself properly. I do all of these things for you, and when it's over, what do you say? Thank you? Thanks for supporting me? No. You have to criticize how I'm *standing*. You had something to say about my *posture*."

"Oh right," I say. "Because you were standing weird. You were standing like a little choir boy —"

"*What!?*" he says with sudden violence. "What did you just say?"

"I said you were standing there like a —"

"Like a little *choir boy*?"

I step back, amazed by how angry he is. "Yeah," I say sheepishly. "I thought it was weird."

"This is the deal, Maddie." He's actually shaking, he's so mad. His lower lip is quivering. "I'm done with you. No more lunch. No more going places. No more helping you out. You suck as a friend, you know that? You're mean and you're selfish and . . . and I'm done with you. Good-bye."

I stand there in utter disbelief. I don't have a clue what just happened. I stand there as he walks back to his nerd buddies.

I probably shouldn't refer to them as his "nerd buddies."

That's probably exactly what he's talking about.

And so I go from two friends, to one friend, to zero friends.

I am back to where I started, back to the library at lunch, back to eating baby carrots at my locker.

I think about what Martin said, of course. But I don't feel capable of doing anything about it. Maybe someday I'll be able to apologize to people in situations like this. Maybe someday I won't even get into situations like this.

But that someday is not now.

Then, as if to fill the friendship void, Emily Brantley starts sniffing around me again. She says hi to me a couple times, once in the bathroom, once in the hall.

After school, as I'm walking through the parking lot, she sees me and calls me over to her and her friends. This includes Amanda Davidson and Petra Brubaker, two popular juniors.

I'm a little nervous, but I let myself be called. I walk over to Amanda's car and we all stare at each other. Emily tells me they're going to a party on Friday, it's people from Bradley Day School. Do I want to come?

I hesitate.

"Don't worry. We'll protect you," she says.

Amanda and Petra have no comment. Then Jake and Alex and Raj drive by in Raj's car. They slow down and talk to us.

"Hey, Maddie," says Jake. "Where've you been hiding?"

"Nowhere," I tell him.

Everyone sort of chitchats for a minute. They talk about parties they went to last weekend. People they hung out with. Fun they had.

As I stand there, I think of Trish going into the ground. I think about the dirt covering her up so she never has to hear about someone else's awesome party weekend ever again.

Lucky her.

I've got a couple days to think about the Bradley Day School party. In the meantime, I've got other things to do. I have school stuff to do. Bizarrely, I feel a need to study.

It's now the end of April, so there's one month of school left. It's a pretty important month. I didn't do too well at the beginning of the semester. So now I decide to try to make it up. Maybe I can pull what would probably be a B-minus average up to an A-minus.

Why I decide to do this, I'm not sure. All that nervous energy, I guess. I gotta put it somewhere. I gotta do something.

The weather doesn't cooperate with my efforts. All the next week, the sun is out, it's warm, and people start showing up at school in shorts and T-shirts. One day, my parents want me to come play tennis with them. My dad tells me I have to relax and enjoy my life more. He wants to take me on a river-rafting trip in June.

I don't want to go river rafting. I want to study. I want to catch up. I hate that my high school transcript is such a total disaster.

I'm a bit of a perfectionist, it turns out. Who knew?

12

Later that week, I'm in my room doing math problems when my mom taps on my door. "Madeline. There's a young man here to see you."

"Is it Martin? Can you tell him —"

"It's not Martin."

I remain frozen for a second. Then I jump out of my chair, run to the window, and look out.

A dirty pickup truck is parked in our driveway.

I run to my closet, kick off my flip-flops, change my shirt, fluff my hair once in the mirror.

I nearly flatten my mother as I race down the hallway . . . then I collect myself to walk down the stairs.

It's him. He's here. Stewart's in my house. Stewart is talking to my *dad.*

"Hey!" says Stewart when he sees me. My dad politely moves away.

"Hey!" I say back. "What are you doing here?"

"I just came up. I had a day off."

"A day off from what?"

"From my job. I work for my dad now."

I grab his hand and lead him out into the front yard. He's wearing carpenter pants, a T-shirt. He looks tanned and healthy. He looks great.

"How did you find me?" I ask.

"Google maps," he says. He smiles at me with that classic Stewart grin. "Is that okay?"

"Of course," I say, squeezing his hand.

"Can we go for a drive?" he asks me.

"Yes!"

We drive around my neighborhood in the pickup. I'm a little embarrassed how posh my street is. But he doesn't seem to notice.

"So I get down there," Stewart tells me, "and I meet my dad. And he's totally different than I remember. He's actually *nice*. And sorta quiet. And then he tells me he's got four years clean and sober. And I'm like, whoa!"

"Oh my God, Stewart. That's great!"

"It's totally great. And he's become this master carpenter. The minute I got there he put me to work. He's the busiest man in Redland!"

I've never seen Stewart so excited.

"You wouldn't believe my life down there . . . we get up at six a.m. every morning . . . and the sun is just coming up and there's dew on the grass . . . there's even a rooster that crows . . . we go to work . . . we build these awesome decks or stairs or hot tub mountings, whatever the people need . . . and at night, I'm so tired, the minute my head hits the pillow I'm out, like that! Talk about healthy living!"

"That sounds amazing!"

"Here's the thing," says Stewart. "I think you should come down there. You should come down and stay with us."

"I'd love to."

"Well, why don't you? I'm serious. You could come down for the summer. Or any time. I'll build us a bed. I've got this little shed next to my dad's cabin. There's a little woodstove and a sink and everything."

"I would love that. But I . . . I think I have to go to summer school."

"Summer school? What for?"

"So I can graduate."

He looks at me funny then. "But we could be together. We could sleep together every night. You could help us build decks. You totally could. Can you hammer a nail?"

"I don't know. I never tried."

"Seriously, Maddie, it's like paradise down there. I went fishing with my dad. We went way up in the mountains and caught fish and cooked them on a little fire. Right there beside the stream. But the whole time, all I was thinking was, I wish Maddie was here. Everything I do, I think about you being there. I want to take you places. I want to show you stuff."

It does sound great. It sounds like the greatest thing ever. But it's not really possible. Doesn't Stewart know that?

"Maybe I can come down after summer school," I tell him. "Maybe for like a week in August."

"But why can't you come down right now?"

"Because I have to finish school. I've totally screwed it up and I'm trying to fix it."

"But if you were in Redland, it wouldn't matter. I thought that's what you wanted? For us to be together?"

"But, Stewart, you made the decision to go down there by yourself. You didn't ask me. You just decided."

"Is there someone else?"

"No! Of course not. Who else could there be? It's just, I have stuff I have to finish. I'm still in high school. I'm not even eighteen yet."

Stewart looks away. "I think about you all the time."

"I know. I do too. But maybe . . ."

"What?"

I take a deep breath and I say it: "Maybe for now we both have to take care of certain things."

There's a long silence.

"I'm sorry," he says. "This was stupid. Driving up here, thinking you could just walk away from your parents . . . your nice house . . ."

"It's not that. It's school. I really want to fix that. I want to be able to do stuff when I get older. Go to college. Get a job."

"Then that's what you should do."

"I still want to see you. I always want to see you. I would move down there in two seconds. I just have to do this first."

An hour later, I'm standing in my driveway. I kiss him one last time, through the window of the pickup. Then I step back and watch him steer backward out the driveway.

Once he's gone, I go back inside. My parents are waiting for me.

"So that's Stewart," I say.

"He seems nice," my mom says politely. "What did he want? Just to say hi?"

"He wanted me to move to Redland and live with him in a little shack in the mountains."

My parents stare at me, bewildered.

"I know," I tell them. "That's what I said."

go to Emily's party. I drive myself in my mom's Volvo, so I can escape if I need to. I park behind Emily's car down the street and walk in with her and Petra and Amanda.

I haven't been to a real party since I got out of Spring Meadow.

This is a real party.

There are hot boys everywhere. In fact, there are no un-hot boys. Bradley Day School is a private school, so not only are they hot, they're well dressed and smart and they're ready to party their asses off.

The house is big with a large, sunken living room and huge windows that look down on the suburbs below. There's music and expensive liquor. People are smoking pot on the deck.

I follow my crew into the kitchen. We make ourselves drinks, with the help of a boy named William, whose house it is and who's got the charm on full blast.

"All right, ladies, what can I do you for?"

"Tequila sunrise," says Petra.

"Rum and Coke," says Amanda. "And I'll make it myself."

"*I* will make it. I'm the host here," says William, grabbing the rum bottle from Amanda. He makes a big show of being the bartender.

I hide behind Emily and then pour myself a glass of orange juice and put some ice cubes in it. I avoid talking to William. I avoid everyone pretty much.

We walk around. Petra and Amanda go talk to William some more and Emily and I end up standing on the deck. Two cute guys immediately come talk to us.

The more aggressive one starts talking to Emily. The other one stands there. He's wearing a Dartmouth T-shirt so I say, "Do you know someone who goes to Dartmouth?"

"Nah, I just got the shirt," he says. He drinks some of his beer and checks out my breasts. He seems interested in them.

"Whatcha drinkin'?" he asks me.

"Orange juice."

"Orange juice and what?"

"Just orange juice," I say.

"No vodka in it?"

"No."

"Oh," he says. But I can see his disappointment. If I'm not getting drunk, how is he going to get to my breasts? He sees someone else he knows, waves and walks away.

I wonder what Martin is doing at this moment. Probably solving advanced calculus problems in his basement. And yet, if I could beam myself into Martin's basement at that moment, I probably would.

Around eleven, a bunch of new people arrive. The party really kicks in then. People are dancing in the living room, crowding into smaller rooms, making out in corners.

It's extremely weird to be sober in the midst of it. It's like I'm watching everything on TV. Then there's a commotion near the front door. I don't see what it is exactly, but the tone of the party suddenly changes. Someone important has arrived. All the attention shifts to the front door area. It's two girls. They cross the room with several boys following behind. The lead girl is actually hiding under her hat as if she were a celebrity.

"Those two girls are causing quite a stir," I say to Emily.

"Tell me about it," she answers.

"Who are they?"

"Who do you think," she says, shaking her head. "It's my sister."

"*That's* your sister?" I say.

"Ashley Brantley. In the flesh."

But Ashley's appearance turns out to be brief. She quickly disappears into some inner sanctum. Everyone kind of buzzes for a moment, and then the party gets back to normal. I dance some with Emily, but I'm getting bored and I tell Emily I have to go. She doesn't want me to. She wants to go find the boys we were talking to on the deck. The Dartmouth boy liked me, she claims, and she likes his friend.

So I hang out a little longer. For her. We walk around the house, but we can't find the boys. We try upstairs.

This is where we stumble upon Ashley in a small study. We open a door and find her and six other extremely cool underclassmen, passing around a mirror of cocaine. They are not happy to be interrupted. "Ever heard of knocking?" a girl says.

"It's okay," says Ashley from the center of the room. "It's my sister."

Emily and I stand in the doorway. One of the guys gestures anxiously for us to come in and shut the door.

We do.

Against my better judgment, I find myself sitting down with Emily. Nobody's very excited we're here, but they're not kicking us out either.

Emily tries to talk to Jayna, one of Ashley's friends. But she doesn't seem to hear. Nobody is listening to anyone. They're all too busy watching the coke go around. Everyone watches a heavily eyelashed girl snort a line.

I know the drill. I've been in a lot of rooms like this.

I look over at Ashley. She's so stoned and drunk and coked up her eyes are shiny slits. But even still, she's so unearthly gorgeous you can't help but stare.

"Oh God, I lost my beer!" she giggles, her hat falling sideways off her head. A boy offers her his.

The people here have no interest in me or Emily. We are in the way. I wait for Emily to make up an excuse and get us out of there. But she's drunk now too. And she wants some cocaine.

It's probably time for me to go home. In fact, I know it is.

But just then, Ashley sees me and blurts out, "Hey look, it's Maddie who went to rehab!"

Every face in the room turns. I can feel the eyes burning into me.

"She's a legend," Ashley says to the boy sitting next to her. "Mad Dog Maddie. She partied so hard they had to lock her up!"

I say nothing.

"Seriously, though, what was that like?" Ashley asks me in front of everyone.

"Not that exciting," I say.

"Well, get her some coke!" says one of the boys.

Everyone agrees this is a good idea and instantly the coke mirror — with the straw, the razor blade, and several rows of white lines — is in front of me. A fresh beer comes with it.

For a moment, I swoon . . . the sight of it, the smell of it . . . I actually feel high for a second, just from looking at it . . . just from having it so close to my face.

But then I recover.

"No," I say. "Actually I'm good."

"She's not partying right now," says Emily in my defense, taking the mirror away from me.

"She's retired!" laughs Ashley. "The legend retires!"

Everyone laughs. Emily positions the straw in her nose and leans over the mirror. Both of the white lines disappear like magic. She leans back, squeezes her nostrils with her fingers. The boy next to her takes the mirror and does two lines. There is a lot of coke here. Probably a thousand dollars worth, at least.

I need to not be here. That is obvious.

I say something about the bathroom. I get up, step over Emily, and make it out the door.

thought I was doing okay. I thought I was handling myself. But once I'm out of that room, my whole body starts to shake. I can barely breathe. I feel like I'm having a heart attack.

There are people in the hallway. I look for somewhere private to go. I find a small bathroom at the end of the hall. I lock myself into it. I collapse onto the toilet.

I lay my head down on my lap. I take deep breaths. I stare at the floor.

I need to call someone.

I dig out my cell phone. I scroll through my numbers. Who can I call? Cynthia, my old counselor? Where is her number? I deleted it.

I look at the other numbers . . . Stewart's mom's . . . Trish . . . Emily . . . Martin . . .

I call Martin. He doesn't answer. I text him: I KNOW UR MAD. AND IM REALLY SORRY. I NEED UR HELP. PLEASE CALL ME.

I put away my phone, lower my head, and shut my eyes. How am I going to get out of here?

But after a few minutes, I regain my composure. *I can do this,* I tell myself. I stand up straight, unlock the door, and begin my journey through the house to my car.

It's not that hard, it turns out. It's not hard at all. I slide by people in the hall, step over people on the stairs. I even say good-bye to Amanda Davidson, who is getting felt up on the front steps outside.

"Leaving so soon?" she says, forcing the boy's hands down.

"Yup."

part four

O n May 21 my dad and I have an official appointment to meet Principal Brown after school. This is to figure out summer school, and see where everything stands.

We follow Mr. Brown into his office. He's round, balding, and has hair growing inside his ears. Today, he looks embarrassed and slightly irritated by the sight of me. He has no right to be like this. I have been a model student for two months. I guess it's the two years before that he's remembering.

Still, we're all here for the same reason: to figure out how to get Maddie Graham graduated and out of Evergreen High School forever.

Mr. Brown takes a seat at his desk and looks me up on his computer.

"Looks like everything's going well for you, Maddie," he says. "No attendance problems. You're still behind in your credits. But your grades look . . . hmmm . . . Well, look at that. Straight As this term. That's great, Maddie. That's very impressive."

I smile. My dad pats my hand.

"I assume you want to graduate? We're not thinking about a GED anymore?"

I nod.

"Good," he says, scrolling down. "Looks like you can graduate with your class if we can make up some credits over the summer."

"That's what I want to do," I say.

"If Maddie could graduate with her class, we would be thrilled," echoes my dad.

Mr. Brown finds some summer school catalogs in his front drawer and hands them to us. "If she's willing to put in the work, there shouldn't be a problem."

"I am," I say without hesitation. "I totally am."

My dad and I flip through the catalogs. Mr. Brown gives me the rundown on my distribution requirements: What classes I have to take. What choices I have. Not that many, it turns out.

When we're done, Mr. Brown asks if we have any questions.

"I don't think so," says my dad.

"Good," says Mr. Brown, turning off his computer.

"Can I say something?" I ask.

"By all means," says Mr. Brown.

I look at him. I look at my dad.

"I want to go to a good college," I say.

Mr. Brown smiles politely. "Well, now, Madeline —"

"I know, Mr. Brown. I've screwed things up," I say. "But I'm serious. I'm going to have a 3.6 this semester. And I'll work my ass off in summer school. I want you to help me go to a good college."

My father looks at me with surprise.

Mr. Brown frowns. "Unfortunately you won't have the same options a normal student would have."

"I understand that," I say. "Maybe I can't go to Harvard. But I can go somewhere, right? Maybe back east? Could you help me do that?"

My father watches me. "We will, honey. Of course we will —"

"Because you can talk to them, right?" I say directly to Mr. Brown. "You can tell them I've changed. You can tell them my whole story."

"Well, yes, but that's only if —"

"If I come through," I say. "But I will come through. You saw my grades this semester. I'll do the same thing in summer school, and next year too."

"Yes, that would speak to your favor. . . ." says Mr. Brown.

"So that's the deal, then? I get straight As from now on. You send me to the best college you can get me into. Is it a deal?"

Mr. Brown stares at me.

"Is it a deal?" I say, sticking out my hand for him to shake.

Reluctantly he lifts his hand. "It's a deal."

2

School ends. Stewart doesn't call. Another week passes. Stewart still doesn't call.

After asking me to give up my future and move into a shack in the woods with him, he can't be bothered to *call me*? The world is so strange. And yet, things happen pretty much like you know they will.

On June 14, I drive my mom's car to my first day of summer school at Portland Community College. I park the Volvo station wagon in the mall-sized parking lot and find my way to the registration office in cement building 2C. That's what the campus is, pretty much — a series of square, gray, cement buildings.

My first class is in cement building 3A. It's a plain, bare-walled classroom, plastic desks, fluorescent lights. I sit near the front. Most of the people are older and from foreign countries. The only people my age are two high school rocker chicks who smell like they've been doing bong hits in the parking lot.

This is my English class. Among other things we're going to read *Lord of the Flies,* which I just read, so that's good. I glance back at the rocker girls. One of them has already lost her book list, even though the teacher just gave them to us two minutes ago.

When that class ends, I go to the next. It's remedial American history, and it's more of the same: drab classroom, bored teacher, more people who can't speak English or who reek of pot smoke or are otherwise hindered in their advancement in life.

At lunchtime, I eat by myself in the cafeteria, which is in cement building 2B. It's actually the nicest of the cement buildings. Everything's clean. There are long tables. The food's not bad.

There's also no social pressure. Everyone sits far apart. Nobody talks to anyone else.

It's okay here. I can do this for eight weeks. But this is not where I belong. I need to go to a real college.

And that's what I'm going to do.

3

To make sure I ace every summer school class, I set up a little work desk in my basement away from the summer sunshine and the fresh-cut grass and the sound of neighbor kids playing basketball in their driveway. I study two hours every night, no matter what. My parents think I have gone insane.

Then one day, when I'm done with homework, I try calling Martin again. I've called him a couple times, but he never calls me back.

This time I call his parents' landline. His mom answers and remembers me from Trish's funeral. She says she'll go get him.

Since his mom is right there, he takes the call. He acts annoyed and put out. I ask him if he wants to go to the mall, maybe go see a movie.

"I thought you didn't like movies."

"Or we could just drive around or whatever," I say.

He sighs loudly and makes a big show of what an inconvenience this is. But he probably has nothing going on either. So he agrees to come by.

I sit outside on my yard so he won't have to wait. He shows up twenty minutes late, but I don't say a word. We drive around. I am glad to be with him. I find his company relaxing. Still, there's something about Martin that brings out my inner smart-ass. It's hard to not use the word "dork" repeatedly in his presence. I make sure to keep my mouth shut.

We end up at the mall, and then go ice-skating, which I still can't do, but I'm better than last time. I get so I can push off a little. And turn. At one point I do almost a whole lap around the rink, teetering like an old lady. Then I crash into the wall.

While I'm trying to do a second lap, Martin gets a call on his cell phone. He hustles off the ice and runs to one of the benches to take it.

Who could that be?

Later, as we're driving home, I ask him who called.

"No one," he says.

"It couldn't have been no one. I've never seen you move so fast."

"Her name is Grace," he says.

"It's a *she*? It's a girl?"

"That's right. And I would appreciate it if you could restrain your acid tongue."

"Okay, okay," I say. "So where'd you meet her?"

"You're sort of the last person I want to talk to about this."

"I'm still a girl, Martin. I like to hear about these things."

"Debate," he says. "We met on the debate team."

"Oh my God. She out-debated you. And now you're in love."

"For your information, I haven't lost a debate in two years."

"You're so smart."

He shakes his head and powers down his window.

"So what's she like?" I say as the car fills with wind.

"She's a girl. That's what she's like."

"But what about her personality?"

He sighs. "I would prefer not to discuss it."

"What kind of clothes does she wear?"

"She wears girls' clothes. I'm not talking to you about her, Maddie. Can you please just accept that?"

"Okay, okay. Jeez," I say.

But that doesn't last.

Four days later, Martin calls me back. I'm eating popcorn with my dad, watching Laser Cats on *Saturday Night Live*. I see his name on my phone and answer.

"Maddie," he says, all nervous and breathless. "It's me, Martin. I have to ask you something."

"Yeah? What is it?"

"It's, uh . . . well . . . do you promise you won't laugh?"

"I won't laugh," I say, licking the popcorn off my fingers.

"Do you promise?"

"Yes."

"And you promise you won't give me a bunch of crap either?"

"What is it, Martin?"

"Well . . . the thing is . . . I'm with Grace. We're at the mall."

"Yes?"

"We're kinda . . . on a date."

"Okay."

"Here's the thing, though . . . I want to kiss her."

"You what?"

"*I want to kiss her.* But I don't know how, exactly. What do I do?"

"Are you serious?"

"Yes, I'm serious," he hisses into the phone. "What do I do?"

"Just reach over and do it."

"Like, just reach over?"

"Well, yeah. And hug her. You know."

"That's it?"

"And be romantic. Go slow."

"Shit," he says. I can hear the mall music in the background. "I've never kissed a girl before."

"And how old are you?"

"Don't start with me, Maddie. Just help me out for once."

"Okay, okay."

I hear the music playing while Martin thinks. "What do I say? Do I ask her?"

"No. Definitely don't ask her."

"How about my breath?"

"Your breath is fine. Don't buy any breath mints. That looks nerdy."

"Do I wait until I take her home?"

"No. It looks lame if you wait until the end. Every guy tries to kiss the girl at the end."

"Yeah. Okay."

"Just act normal, relax, and let it happen. Watch her for signs. If she grabs your arm, or touches you, or snuggles up to you in any way. Go for it."

"Okay. Yeah. Definitely."

"And Martin?"

"Yeah?"

"You're cute. So don't worry. She wants to make out with you."

"Really? You think I'm cute?"

"Yeah. Especially lately. You're more confident."

"Really?"

"Yeah."

"In what way?"

"I don't know. You just are. You're more mature."

"Wow," he whispers, amazed at this information. Then he composes himself. "Okay. Cool. I'm totally going to do this. I totally am."

"Good luck."

"Thanks, Maddie."

4

Mid-July, I'm eating lunch in the cafeteria in cement building 2B. I look up and see the two rocker girls from my English class. Their names are Allison and Veronica.

"Can we sit with you?" asks Allison.

"Yeah, we're bored with each other," says Veronica.

"Sure," I say.

They plop down on their chairs. Allison salts her salad. Veronica covers her large order of French fries with ketchup.

"Oh my God, I am so sick of summer school," says Veronica.

"How can you stand to sit in the front?" Allison asks me.

I shrug.

"You sure are smart," says Veronica. She wears a black hoodie with millions of tiny skulls on it.

"Yeah, you know all the answers," says Allison.

"I had to miss some school. So I try to study," I tell them.

"I never study. I hate homework," says Allison, eating her salted salad. "I don't even understand homework. Why can't we just do it in class?"

"I hate books," says Veronica. "I can't even read. That's what they finally figured out. I have a learning disability."

"You can read a little," says Allison.

"Oh, I can read, like, signs and stuff," says Veronica.

"You can read *Us Weekly*," says Allison.

They sit there across from me, noisily munching their food.

"So what's your deal?" asks Allison.

"Yeah, we've been wondering," says Veronica.

"Do you have a boyfriend?"

"Yeah, what's your guy situation?"

They both stare at me, waiting for the answer to this all-important question.

"I wouldn't call him a boyfriend," I answer. "It's kind of a long-distance thing at the moment."

"Oh, that sucks," says Allison. "Those never work."

"They cheat on you," says Veronica. "That's what happened to me."

"Where is he?" asks Allison.

"He's in Redland," I answer.

"Where's that?"

"Down south. Near California."

"That's not good," says Allison. "Girls in California will steal your man."

"They all got fake boobs."

"Guys like fake boobs," Veronica tells me. "They say they don't. But they do. The bigger the better."

"I knew this girl," says Allison. "She got these huge ones. For her birthday. Her parents got them for her."

"That's so creepy," says Veronica. "Like when your *dad* pays for them."

They both pause to eat for a minute.

"You gonna marry him?" Allison asks.

"Probably not," I tell them. "I'm only seventeen."

"Hey, when you're young is when you get the best guys," says Allison. "You might as well grab a good one while you can."

"Maybe you could get pregnant," says Veronica.

I look at the two of them. "Yeah, maybe," I say.

"Guys are like buses," says Allison. "Why get on the first one you see, when there's another one coming right after? Or something like that. Or maybe it's the opposite. I heard that on *Oprah*."

We all nod at the wisdom of *Oprah*. They eat their French fries. I eat my yogurt. Then they have to go, so they can smoke before class.

I say good-bye and watch them go.

I have to go to a good college, I tell myself.

5

I ace my first round of tests at summer school. Straight As. All the way across.

I find this out in the computer room in cement building 3F. I walk into the hot sun and take a long deep breath of relief.

Then I call Martin and insist that he come celebrate with me, or at least take me out for ice cream. He can't. He and Grace are going to the movies. He says I can come with them if I want.

This probably isn't the smartest idea, but I say yes. I have to do something social for once.

Martin picks me up at my house. Grace is sitting in the front seat of his car. I recognize her from school. She's one of those prissy, smart girls I would never talk to in a million years. She is sort of cute, though. I have to give Martin credit for that. It's surprising how cute she is.

We drive along. Grace doesn't say anything. Neither does Martin. So I have to talk. I tell them about my lunch with Allison and Veronica at community college.

"It sounds like their parents haven't exposed them to the right things," says Grace, which is the polite thing to say.

I want to say something really harsh and brutal and hilarious, but for Martin's sake I keep my mouth shut.

Grace. Wow.

We get to the movie. It's called *Free Fall* and it's about magazine writers in New York having relationships, falling in love, dining in fancy restaurants.

The characters all talk endlessly about themselves.

For a minute I think: *Maybe college isn't so great, if it turns you into these people.*

But no, it's just a movie.

Afterward, we get ice cream. Grace wants to talk about the magazine business, since a friend of her mom's works for a magazine in New York.

"It isn't really like that," Grace says. "They always try to make it seem more glamorous. My father is an eye doctor and, trust me, it is not at all like *Grey's Anatomy.*"

Martin finds everything Grace says fascinating. I don't. But I'm happy for him. They drop me off first so they can go make out somewhere.

Martin has told me they make out constantly. And that Grace wants to "experiment with petting."

That's probably what they do after they drop me off.

Experiment with petting.

Summer continues. One day, I wander into the community college counseling office and look at their college brochures. They have a little box for the Eastern colleges, at the bottom of a bookshelf.

I look at them. They are beautiful brochures. And the schools all sound so distinguished: Smith. Swarthmore. Wellesley. Haverford. I remember Smith because that's where Sylvia Plath went in *The Bell Jar*, the novel everyone read in rehab.

I bring several of the brochures home and look at them with my mom. She doesn't think I could go somewhere "prestigious," but then, she doesn't know much about it. She went to Southern Oregon State, where they teach you what fertilizer to use on your alfalfa crop. But my dad, who went to MIT, is surprised when he sees them on the table. He gets all excited. He dated a "Smithie" once, he tells me. From the light in his eyes, I assume it was a satisfactory experience.

Nothing else very interesting happens. Stewart finally calls a couple times. He wants me to come down, for the week after summer school ends.

But no sooner do we start to make a plan, then he vanishes again. After a week of no contact, I try calling him at the various numbers I have. None of them work. I even call his sister's number, which I have for some reason. She's glad I called; she's heard great things about me. As for Stewart, she only knows what I know — that he's living in a shed behind his dad's house — his dad, who apparently doesn't even have a landline.

I'm not mad. I'm not disappointed. I just want to talk to him. I miss him.

I call Emily Brantley and she's excited to hear from me but she is at that moment sunbathing on a sailboat in the San Juan Islands. Her whole family is there for two weeks. Her sister, Ashley, has already been caught fooling around with the thirty-year-old deckhand. It's a big scandal. She promises to call me as soon as she gets back and tell me the gory details.

So I go back to what I was doing. Studying. I also start reading this book about Sylvia Plath and her marriage to Ted Hughes, who was British and insane and horrible to her. Every afternoon after school I drive to this vegan tea shop and sit in the courtyard reading. At night, I drive around in my mom's Volvo and listen to *Loveline* on the radio.

One night, I drive downtown and have an iced coffee at Metro Café. I see the street kids hanging out. Jeff Weed is there. And Bad Samantha. And a bunch of new people I've never seen before.

I couldn't hang with those people now. For starters, I dress too normal. And what would I even say to them?

I hope I don't become some boring slag. *You sound like somebody's wife.* Stewart actually said that to me. And he meant it.

The Sunday before finals I do a complete review of all of my summer school classes. And then my phone rings.

Pretty much my whole social life this summer has been over the phone, so that's not unusual. But it's weird that anyone would call now. Everyone knows I have finals tomorrow.

I pick it up. It's Stewart. *Now* he calls. But whatever, I'm not going to be angry.

"Hey," I say calmly.

"Hey."

"Long time, no see. Or no talk."

"Sorry. I been kinda . . . busy."

I say nothing. I scribble in the margins of my biology book.

"Are you done with summer school?" he asks. His voice sounds strange, like he just woke up.

"Almost," I say.

"You gonna come down here when you're done?"

"I don't know if that's a good idea. Since you keep disappearing."

"I need you, though."

"What do you need me for?"

"I need you because . . . I just do."

This is weird. Stewart doesn't sound like himself.

"How's your dad?" I ask.

"He's okay."

"Are you still building decks?"

"Not right at the moment."

"How come?"

"We kinda . . . had a disagreement."

"What about?"

"Different things."

I scribble more.

"Maddie," he says. "There's something I gotta tell you."

"Yeah?"

"I'm not really doin' too good."

"What do you mean?"

"I'm kinda drunk."

"You are? Right now?"

"Uh-huh."

I'm caught off guard by this information. I struggle to think of the logical next question. "You're drunk? Like drunk on alcohol?"

"Yeah. Pretty much."

I stop scribbling. "Where are you?"

"Uh . . . outside a bar? I met some people. That's kinda how it started."

"Oh, Stewart," I say.

"I . . . I'm so tired. That's the thing. We've been partyin' for, like, four days straight."

"How did it happen?"

"I dunno. It just did."

I can't think of what to say back.

And then I hear him crying. I can hear him sobbing away from the phone.

"Maddie?" he finally says.

"Yeah?"

"What do I do? I don't know what to do."

I don't know what to do either. My brain begins to churn. I start to think through the options. "Okay . . ." I say into the phone. "Stewart . . . listen to me. Tell me where you are. Tell me exactly where you are. . . ."

8

"**D**ad? Can I talk to you?"

My dad is in his office. He's doing something on his computer.

"Sure, honey. You ready for your tests?"

I nod. I try to smile. "As ready as I'll ever be."

He hears something in my voice and glances up at me. He sees the urgency in my face. "Come in, Maddie. What is it?"

I take a seat in the chair across from him. I think for a second before I speak. "You know that guy Stewart, who came here?"

"Yeah, sure."

I take a deep breath.

"What's up?" asks my dad. "Where is he?"

"He's in Redland."

"What's he doing down there?"

"He went to live with his dad. It seemed to be working out for him. But now it looks like it's not."

My dad watches me from his big, leather chair.

"He's in trouble," I say. "And he needs my help. I have to go get him."

"When?"

"Right now. Tonight."

"But you have your summer school finals tomorrow."

"I know."

"Are you going to reschedule?"

"I don't think you can do that. But if I leave now, I can get there and be back by morning. I can make it by a couple hours."

"But, honey, you can't drive down to Redland in the middle of the night. You need to sleep. You can't take final exams on no sleep."

"I think I can do it."

"But, honey, seriously, why would you? What about your deal with Mr. Brown?"

"I know, I know."

He watches my face. "Is there more to this than you're telling me?" he asks. "This Stewart — are you in love with him?"

I avoid his gaze. "Yes. I mean, I was. I mean, I don't know exactly. The thing is, I haven't always been a great friend to people."

"You can't blame yourself for Trish, Madeline."

"Dad. If something happens to Stewart, and I didn't do *everything* I could to help him, I would never forgive myself. Ever."

He stares at me. "Maddie, I know what you're saying. But at some point you have to ask yourself: Is it worth it? Are these the kind of people you want in your life going forward?"

"I know, Dad. But he needs help now. And I can help him. And that's what I'm going to do."

My dad sighs. "Honey, I don't think I can let you."

"Dad, I don't think you can stop me."

He stares at me for a minute, then shakes his head. "No, I suppose not."

shift into fourth gear and hit the interstate doing eighty in my dad's new BMW. I drive like that the whole way. I shave a half hour off the drive time and pull off at the Redland exit at 12:15 a.m. I follow the GPS down the main street of the town and onto a dark stretch of road beyond. Finally, in the middle of nowhere, I come to the Hungry Bear Saloon. A dozen cars and pickups are parked in front. A neon Pabst Blue Ribbon sign glows in the window. I slow down and ease into the parking lot. The dusty gravel is bathed in the light of a full summer moon.

I park and get out of my dad's BMW. The other cars are not BMWs. They are old trucks, newer trucks, clunker cars, clunker vans. An old Volkswagen bus is disintegrating in a dirt field across the street.

I walk behind the parked cars, looking for Stewart. I told him to stay outside. I pass the front of the building and the door suddenly bursts open. Drunk people come spilling out, laughing and nearly tumbling down the wooden steps. I stay out of their way. I continue to move through the parking lot. I see no sign of Stewart. I told him to stay outside. And not to leave with the other people. Did he do it?

I only know Stewart sober. I don't know him drunk. What will he do? I have no idea.

I walk farther, circling around to the side of the building. Here I encounter a dumpster, an old sink, a bunch of empty kegs stacked against the wall. I keep going around the building and find that there's another parking lot in back. It's empty, but there's an old station wagon at the far end. It has two flat tires and is parked under some trees. One of the back doors is open slightly.

I walk quickly, quietly across the gravel. I approach the car, open the back door, and there's Stewart. He's lying on the backseat, passed out. His hair is longer than when I last saw him. He has the straggly beginnings of a beard.

I grip the toe of his booted foot. I'm going to wake him up, but then I don't.

I stare at him instead. I listen to the sounds of the forest all around me. This is the boy I love. And I do love him. More than anything. But what's going to happen to him? I hear distant voices from the front of the saloon. A car starts somewhere. I hear it reverse, pull away.

And what about me? Am I the kind of person who comes running to save people like Stewart for the rest of my life?

I kinda don't think so.

Maybe this is it for Stewart and me. Maybe tonight is the end.

Then I hear a truck behind me. It's coming around the building and is turning into the back parking lot.

This might complicate things.

I watch the truck's headlights sweep across the gravel, passing over me and the abandoned car.

They see me. They drive forward, apparently curious to see who the girl is in the back of the parking lot in the middle of the night. I yank on Stewart's foot. "Stewart, wake up," I whisper. *"Stewart!"*

It's a work truck, it's beat-up. It has big side compartments for tools. It rolls to a stop beside me. "Hello," says the driver from the cab. A little cloud of dust drifts by.

"Hello," I say back.

"Whatcha doin'?" he asks. I can see there are two men in the cab of the truck.

"Nothing," I say. "Just my friend here. He had a little too much tonight."

"There's somebody in that car, look," the passenger whispers to the driver.

"He's okay," I say. "I'm going to take him home."

I shake Stewart's foot again. *"Stewart!"* I say under my breath.

They whisper to each other for a moment. Then they shut off the truck. A weird chill of fear slides down my spine. The truck is between me and the back of the saloon. I am hidden from view.

The doors open. The two men get out.

It's very quiet now. Very dark. Their boots are loud in the gravel. The passenger comes around the truck to get a better look at me. They both glance around the deserted parking lot.

"Does your friend there still got his pants on?" says the driver.

"Yes. Of course. He just had to lie down for a second," I say. "He's just waking up."

"He don' look like he's wakin' up to me."

The two men are not here to help. They both wear greasy baseball caps. One has long, graying hair. They are ugly men and I can read the ugly thoughts on their faces.

"Really, it's fine," I stammer. "I can handle it."

"You 'spect us to believe you ain't makin' a little money back here?" says the passenger.

"No. I'm . . . I'm a friend."

"I'm sure you are, girly."

They move forward. I step back. They both stare at Stewart's inert body.

The passenger leans forward and looks in the car window. "Yeah, I'd say he's done for the night."

"You got his wallet?" the driver asks.

"No, I told you. I'm a friend. I'm taking him home."

They turn and look at me. "How much you charge anyway?"

"It's not like that. I'm in high school."

"You don't look like you're in high school."

I back away more. I try to think. What do I have? Keys. My phone. What else? Nothing.

"I'll give you twenty bucks, girly."

"No, thank you," I say.

"Why not make a little money?" says the driver. "We could probably just take it for free anyway."

I've now backed up enough that I can see the saloon. But it's far away. I'll scream. I try to get a breath, but I'm so scared. I can't get any air, I can't fill my lungs —

They look at each other. They attack.

They're fast. Faster than I'm ready for. They have me in one quick dash. The passenger tackles me and slams me to the ground. He smells like sweat and oil and whiskey.

The driver grabs my belt buckle. I kick him.

"Stewart!" I cry. I manage to roll over. I get to my knees. But the passenger has his arm around my neck. Then the other one lands on me from behind, driving me back into the ground. The passenger slaps his thick hand over my mouth. I bite it.

"Ahhhh!" he yells.

"Shhhhh!" hisses his friend.

"Stew —!!!" I scream, but hardly anything comes out.

They hold me down. They snarl at me, breathe on me. I twist and fight and then one of them jams his knee into my neck. My face is ground into the dust. My mouth fills with gravel.

They've got me. Facedown. They've got my belt undone. I can feel my jeans giving way. I try to twist around, but I'm completely pinned.

They yank my jeans down to my knees. My skin is exposed. The sensation is terrifying. I fight more, try to scream, twist, kick —

I feel my underwear rip. I manage to get my neck free. I twist onto my side.

Then there's a new sound: A door slams somewhere.

"Hey! *Hey!*" a woman's voice calls out. "What the hell is goin' on back there!?"

The men freeze. Then they release me. They jump up and run to their truck. I can see a woman in an apron, standing at the back door of the saloon.

"Who is that?" she says, staring at the truck as it peels out and tears around the building.

In a cloud of dust, I spit dirt and gravel out of my mouth. I roll over and try to pull my pants up. The top button is ripped out.

The woman takes a few steps into the parking lot. "You're not allowed back here," she says. "This is private property."

I get my pants up. I spit blood out of my mouth.

She comes closer and studies the scene in the dark. She sees Stewart's foot.

"That's my car!" says the woman. "What's he doin' in my car?"

I get to my feet. I open the door completely and grip Stewart's foot. I pull him out of the car, all the way out, until he lands on his head on the gravel. This wakes him up. He begins to move. His eyes open.

"You stay right there, young lady," says the woman. "I'm calling the sheriff."

Stewart rolls onto his side. He looks around the parking lot, a dull, blank expression on his face. When the woman goes inside, I grab him by the elbow and start pulling him up.

"What's happening?" he says.

"We're leaving. Now."

I help him to his feet. He takes a few unsteady steps. I hold my pants up with my hand and pull him forward.

"Come on!" I hiss at him. "Hurry!"

He begins to move faster. We circle around to the front parking lot and I push Stewart into the BMW. I slam the door. I can hear a commotion now, in the back parking lot. I get in the driver's seat, start the car. The bouncer of the bar appears at the front door. I calmly back out of the parking lot. He sees me and yells something as I shift into first. He runs at the car. I hit the gas hard. The BMW rips forward, fishtailing and spraying him with parking lot gravel.

I drive sixty to the freeway. Beside me, Stewart slowly comes to his senses. On the freeway, he starts to ask me questions. I find I can't really answer him.

I find I can't really look him in the face.

part five

drop off Stewart at his sister's at three in the morning. Six hours later, on three hours' sleep, with a fat lip and bruises everywhere, I take my summer school finals.

I think I do okay. I finish all the questions.

Then I go to my car in the parking lot and cry for two hours.

Later that night, when I see my dad, I resolve to tell him what happened. That's what I have to do, right? But I'm cried out and exhausted and somehow the words won't come.

Besides, I've been lying to my parents about "what happened last night" my whole life. It's not like I know how to tell them such things. Nor do they know how to hear them.

School starts two weeks later. On the first day of my senior year, I go to Mr. Brown's office. He seems genuinely happy to see me. "How was your summer?" he asks me in his office.

"All right," I say.

"And summer school?" he says.

"It was harder than it looked," I say. I hand over my transcript.

He takes it, unfolds it, sits back in his chair. Then he reads my grades out loud: "A, B, A, B-plus."

I sit there, watching him.

"Excellent," he says. "That's very good."

"I know I promised you I'd get straight As," I say, embarrassed.

"You did very well, Madeline. I wouldn't worry about that."

"Yeah, but can I still go to college somewhere good?"

"Honestly? No. But you couldn't have done that anyway. We will do what we can. I've already talked to the college counselor about your situation. She has some excellent ideas for you."

"Thanks," I say.

He continues to read through the transcript. "No absences, no tardies. This is an excellent showing, Maddie. In all my years of teaching, I have never seen anyone turn themselves around quite like you have."

"Thanks," I say again. "The straight As thing, something sort of happened —"

He waves his hand at me. "Don't say another word about it. We're all very proud of you here. We will do everything we can to help."

Then Stewart calls. He wants to meet me downtown. He says he'll take the bus in from Centralia.

I go. It's been almost three weeks since I left him at his sister's.

We meet at a McDonald's by the bus station. He's totally broke. And without his grandmother around, he can't afford Spring Meadow. So he's staying sober without rehab. He's going to AA meetings in Centralia every day. He goes every morning and every night.

He's been sober nineteen days.

"How do you feel?" I ask him.

"Not so great," he says. "I'm sorry you had to see that."

"It happens," I say, staring out the window. "That's what Cynthia always said."

We both drink our coffees. No hot chocolate today.

"What was it like?" I ask him. "Being drunk again?"

He shakes his head. "At first it was the greatest feeling in the world. Like for one instant, everything made sense again. My brain was like: *thank God!*"

"And then?"

"And then everything went to shit."

I nod.

"There's one thing," he says. "That night. What was going on in the parking lot? Someone else was there. Some guys. Were they giving you a hard time?"

"I don't know what they were doing," I say.

Stewart stares at his coffee cup. "That town — what a scene that was. Rednecks on meth. It was messed up."

"You were pretty messed up yourself."

"Yeah. I guess I was." He thinks for a moment. "Thanks for doing that. Coming down there in the middle of the night. I mean it. I know you had your tests and stuff."

"Yeah . . ." I say.

I'm about to say something then, a little speech I've been practicing for days. Something like, *I don't think we should see each other for a while.*

But before I can say anything, I notice something about his hand.

"Your grandmother's ring?" I say. "Where is it?"

"Oh," he says, looking down at his fingers. "I lost it."

"You *lost* it?"

"I know. I'm so pissed. I don't know where it went."

"But how could you do that?"

"I didn't *do* it. It just happened."

"But, Stewart."

"I didn't *mean* to lose it," he says, annoyed.

I touch his bare finger. His whole hand, it looks so exposed.

"I knew you should have kept it," he says. "Then we'd still have it."

I walk him back to the bus station. We sit in the plastic seats and wait for the bus. When it pulls in, we go into the concrete loading area, he kisses me on the cheek. We hold each other. Maybe I don't have to say anything. Maybe he understands we should just be friends for a while.

"I know how it looks," he says to me over the roar of the buses. "It looks like I can't make it. But I can. I will. I'm gonna stay clean this time."

I can't meet his eyes. So I hug him again. I hold him to me. He holds me back, kisses the top of my head.

Then I let him go. And walk away. And go to my car.

And drive.

4

September passes more quickly than ever. One week, it's eighty degrees and the soccer team is running around without shirts. The next week, it's cold and the leaves are changing and there's that familiar burnt-wood smell in the air.

Sitting in study hall, I get bored one day and count up my sober time: a little more than nine months. That's a lot, I realize. It is for me, anyway.

I feel more normal too. I no longer hide out. I eat in the cafeteria. I hang out in the hall. I go from being scary Rehab Girl to being just like any other senior, a little superior but liked and respected anyway. Every senior has some embarrassing story. I'm not so unique.

October comes. I seem to spend most of my free time with Martin and Grace. I'm not sure Grace enjoys my company as much as Martin, but too bad for her. Another guy, Doug Gerrard, who's Martin's friend, also hangs out with us. He appears to like me but does nothing about it. He is content to follow us around, not talk, stare at me when he thinks I'm not looking, lend me pens, give me pieces of gum.

I am now in two AP classes, history and English. I love the teachers in these classes and they love me — a good student they didn't even know they had. I ace my tests. I talk in class. It's kind of fun to shock people.

Another interesting thing that happens as the semester wears on: I become even closer with Emily Brantley. We start to become, dare I say it, best friends. Or at least the best of my *girl*friends, since in a way, Martin is my real best friend.

My friendship with Emily rises to an even higher level when she confides in me that she's not going to drink anymore, at least not from Sunday to Thursday. She says she's sick of people not taking her seriously. She wants to be more like me: serious and mysterious.

This becomes our running joke: *serious and mysterious.* Like I have any secrets left.

Of course, Emily's no-drinking policy doesn't last; she still has to smoke a little weed before school, and she figures a couple beers with Raj and Jake aren't going to hurt anything . . . but for a while she manages it, and we spend a few weekday nights studying together or driving around, eating frozen yogurt. She's actually sort of smart, that's the interesting thing. We're both the same in that way, smart girls who somehow decided we shouldn't be, or were afraid to be, or just decided to rebel against our own abilities for some reason.

Martin changes a lot senior year too. With Grace at his side, he becomes less clueless, more confident, a little more fun. Also, I begin to comprehend how smart he really is. He kills on his SATs and wins every scholarship he tries for. When he applies early admission to Stanford, he gets in, no problem.

I think about that a lot. Martin at Stanford. I'm totally happy for him, of course. But it also makes me sad for myself. No matter what I do now, there are certain doors I have already closed, certain opportunities I'll never get back.

There's nothing to be done, I guess. It is what it is.

The good news is Stewart. He continues to keep himself clean and sober. He begins to call me regularly, to give me updates. He gets three weeks, four weeks, five weeks. He's doing it. He's making it.

He moves into the basement of his new AA sponsor's house. He works a part-time job at a local garage. He sends me e-mails from the Centralia Public Library, telling me about AA and working the Twelve Steps. He talks about God. He talks about "spirituality." He talks about Sober Bowling and hanging out with his sponsor, fixing motorcycles.

We don't see each other in person for nearly a month, and then, one beautiful autumn night, he shows up at my house on a huge Harley-Davidson. We talk in the driveway, under our big maple tree with its bright yellow leaves. Stewart sits on the Harley in his greasy coveralls, his helmet in his hands. I stand there like the schoolgirl I've become, a copy of *Macbeth* under my arm.

I haven't slept with him now since last spring. It seems like a century ago. And yet standing there with him, in the driveway, I love him as much as I ever did. I don't let him know this of course. I can't afford to, really.

I ask him about his life, about Centralia, about his sponsor, and how you adjust the choke on a two-cycle Yamaha engine. I watch his eyes while he describes certain things. I watch his beautiful lips as he talks.

But when he's gone, something happens in my chest and I don't love him. I can't. I don't love anybody.

And that night, as I'm falling asleep, I see the two men behind the Hungry Bear Saloon. I smell their foulness. I feel their clawing hands, tearing at my clothes.

But I put that memory away. I push it down, lock it away, with all the other memories like it. I can't dwell on the past now. I have to study. I have to work. I've already lost so much time. I can't waste one more second of my life on such things.

That's what it seems like anyway. That's the race I seem to be running.

5

Since we're now best friends, Emily asks me to come hang out with these two boys she met over the summer in the San Juan Islands. Paul, the boy she sorta likes, and his friend Simon are seniors from back east. They're in Portland with Paul's dad, checking out Reed College and some other schools out west.

Paul and Simon meet us in the lobby of the Hilton downtown. Paul is handsome and tanned, with curly black hair. He's wearing a pressed white shirt and jeans. "I apologize for the Brooks Brothers shirt," he says immediately. "My dad made me wear it, since that's what people did when they visited colleges in, like, 1982."

The other guy, Simon, wears a T-shirt, jeans, and has medium-length dirty-blond hair. He stands up to meet us — very polite — and then sits back down when we sit.

We talk about colleges for a while. How all the Eastern people want to come west, all the Western people want to go east.

I babble on about how I think Eastern schools are so old and established and steeped in tradition, and I would give anything to go to one. Simon and Paul have a laugh at that. That world is exactly what they're trying to escape from.

Paul has his dad's credit card, so we go to a fancy restaurant. Paul goes through this whole conversation with the waiter about which local wine we should have, which vintage, which vineyard, which year, only to have the waiter — with incredible dignity — inquire as to the actual birth dates of the four of us.

So no wine for us.

Emily loves all this, of course. She and Paul are really warming to each other. When we go to Starbucks afterward, they can't keep their hands off each other as they make fun of the lifestyle CDs at the counter.

After that, we wander around downtown. At Pioneer Square, Paul borrows a skateboard from some unsuspecting local and takes off down the sidewalk on it.

Emily chases after him, shrieking at the top of her lungs. Simon and I stand holding their lattes, while at the end of the block, Paul falls on his ass. Emily runs to him, helps him up, and then gets on the skateboard herself. She then falls and is caught by Paul, who seems to like the feel of her.

"Seems to be a spark," I say to Simon.

"Might even be a flame," he says back.

We hold their lattes and watch Paul and Emily help each other ride the skateboard. There's a lot of touching, groping, giggling . . . and then they kiss.

"Hmmmm," says Simon. "This might take a while."

We take a seat on the brick wall. I look more closely at Simon then. He's cuter than I originally thought.

"So what do you think you'll study in college?" I ask.

"Philosophy."

"Really? Why that?"

"I like to think a lot," he says. "How about you?"

"I don't know. English maybe. I like to read."

"Reading's cool."

"I like following other people's thoughts."

"Yeah, me too. I like if you're reading something, and they're saying something you always thought, but they're putting it in the exact right way."

"Yeah, or like in a novel, if someone describes something a certain way and at first you're like, *what*? But then you're like, *oh, I see.*"

"Yeah," says Simon. "Good metaphors are awesome."

We sit there for a second. I look at Simon. He looks at me.

I think he might like me. Which is weird. Normal people never like me.

6

When Emily and I get in the car to drive home, I don't say a word at first. I don't have to, though, because as soon as we're moving, Emily bursts out laughing hysterically. "Oh my God, I LOVE THAT BOY!"

I'm laughing too. "I thought you guys were gonna do it on the sidewalk."

"I know. He was very grabby, wasn't he? What about Simon — what did you think of him?"

"He was nice."

"Oh, come on! You liked him. He's the perfect guy for you."

"How so?"

"He's smart. He's cool. He stands up when you're introduced to him. You should totally be with a guy like that. No offense to Stewart. But you need someone who's interested in the same things you're interested in."

I don't really have an answer for this.

"Oh my God," says Emily when her phone buzzes in her pocket. "That's probably Paul. He's probably going to want to meet up. . . ."

But it's not Paul.

"Oh Jesus," she says, reading it. "It's my stupid sister."

"What does she want?"

"She's probably wasted someplace. . . ."

Ashley Brantley is indeed wasted someplace. She's at Jayna Rosenfeld's, one of her hot sophomore friends. It's actually Jayna sending the message. Emily calls her, the two have a short conversation, and Emily hangs up.

"Would you mind terribly if we go pick up my sister?" Emily asks me.

"Not at all."

We drive to Jayna's house, where we find Ashley, Jayna, and Rachel in her basement. Ashley is sprawled in a reclining chair with her head lolling back. When we come in, she sits up.

"Hey, you guys," she says in a slightly too-loud voice. "Wudup?"

"C'mon, Ashley," says Emily, who is pissed and does not want her brilliant evening spoiled in this way. "We're taking you home."

Ashley sees me. "Hey, Maddie, what are you doing here? Out partying with my sister?"

Emily doesn't let me answer. "Get up, Ashley. We're leaving."

Ashley doesn't seem that bad . . . until she tries to stand up. "Ooops, I seem to be a little tipsy," she says, laughing. Jayna and Rachel help her steady herself.

We help her out the basement door and onto the wet lawn. We walk her slowly around the house to the street.

"Why are we going this way?" she asks us.

"Because last time you couldn't make it up the stairs," says Emily.

"I can make it," says Ashley. "God, you guys are so uptight."

I say nothing during all of this. I watch as Rachel and Emily help Ashley into my car.

We get her into the backseat. We strap her in. Jayna, who is disgusted, walks away without another word. Rachel, who must be a new friend and is probably still thrilled to be in the presence of superstar Ashley, squeezes her hand and says good-bye.

"Whatever," Ashley replies with contempt.

It's a ten-minute drive to the Brantley residence. Emily directs me away from the driveway and tells me to park in the street. Emily studies the front of the house for signs of her parents' whereabouts.

"I can't deal with Mom and Dad right now," Ashley says from the backseat.

"Well, too bad," says Emily. "'Cause you're gonna have to."

"They'll freak out, and you know it."

Emily studies the house. "They might be in bed," she says to me. "It's almost one."

"Maybe you should go find out," commands Ashley from the backseat.

"Maybe you should shut the fuck up!" Emily snaps, glaring back at her sister.

"Okay, okay. It was just a suggestion."

"I'm sick of covering for you," says Emily. "Okay?"

"I'm sick of covering for me too," mumbles Ashley to herself.

Emily gives me her most exasperated look. "Would you talk to her while I'm gone?" she asks me.

"What do you want me to say?"

"Tell her what happens if you keep getting trashed every night."

216

Emily gets out and quietly shuts the door. She walks quietly, stealthily up her own driveway.

I look at Ashley in the rearview mirror. "Hey, Ashley," I say.

"What?"

"Bad things happen if you keep getting trashed every night."

"Yeah? Like what?" she says.

"Lots of things."

"Name one."

"You could get raped," I say.

"So?"

"You could get killed."

"I don't care if I die."

"You could get pregnant."

"I'll get an abortion."

I find her in the rearview mirror. "People stop thinking you're cool," I say. "And they start thinking you're a pathetic loser."

"So? They already think that now."

I'm surprised by that. "Do they?"

"They're starting to."

"Okay, well, that's what happens. I've done my duty. The lecture is over."

I lean forward and turn on the radio.

"I do have one queshion, though," she says, slurring her words slightly. "What's it like in rehab? Like, what do you do all day?"

I wasn't expecting any questions. I look back into the mirror. "You sit around. And talk."

"That sounds boring," she says.

"It is."

I go back to the radio.

"Were there other high school people?" she interrupts.

"There were a few."

"Were there boys?"

"There were, but you can't hook up with them."

"Why not?"

"Because boys tend to be part of the problem."

She laughs. "They got that right."

I tune the radio.

"Whaddaya do at night?" she says. "In re-*hab*?"

"Nothing," I say. "Watch TV. Play cards. They had a thing called movie night. That was your big chance to hit the town."

"Movie night," she says. "God, it sounds awful."

"Actually, movie night was sort of fun. I used to go with this other girl, Trish. We used to dress up."

"How old was Trish?"

"Eighteen."

"Where is she?"

"She's dead."

"Well, *that* sucks."

"People die," I say, finding Ashley's face in the mirror. "That part's true. It really happens."

"I know," she says, letting her head rest back on the seat. "You don't have to tell me."

I say nothing more. I tune the radio and then I see Emily sneaking back down the driveway. She opens Ashley's door. "You lucked out this time. Mom and Dad are asleep."

"Yeah, yeah," says Ashley, kicking her way out of the car. "Lucky me."

Stewart invites me to come to his AA meeting in Centralia on Saturday. He's getting his sixty-day coin. He wants me to be there, to help celebrate.

I drive the fifty-seven miles to Centralia and follow his directions to the meeting. It's in a modest wooden church with a muddy, potholed parking lot. I park and step around the puddles and go inside.

The group is small, about twenty people sitting around in folding chairs. They are mostly older people: farmers, house-wives, people who work at the local lumber mill. It's cozy, friendly. They have coffee in one of those big silver pots.

I take a seat in one of the metal chairs. The first thing I notice is how much the local people love Stewart. His sixty days is all anyone talks about. It's an accomplishment they all share. He's their mascot, their pet project. He belongs to them now. He's their Lost Prince.

Stewart is embarrassed by all the attention. But he likes it, you can tell. And he loves these people back in his simple way. You can see it in his eyes.

After the meeting, the group takes him out to dinner at the

one Chinese restaurant in downtown Centralia. I go along, the one stranger in the group. Stewart walks with me, introduces me to people, keeps me at his side.

At the restaurant, people toast him with their Diet Cokes and water glasses. Stewart stands up and thanks everyone. It's a fun little party. Even knowing no one, I have a great time.

Later, when everyone is gone, Stewart and I walk through silent Centralia, back to the church parking lot to my car. It's a little weird being alone with him. I feel jealous of the Centralia people. I wish I had Stewart in my life.

"Thanks for coming down," he says when we reach my car.

"I was glad to come," I say, looking at my car keys. "I'm glad you're doing well."

"You know," he says, "I've been thinking about moving up to Portland."

I look up with surprise.

"I can't live in a basement forever," he says, grinning.

I grin too. He's watching me, staring down at me like he does. His eyes are blazing.

He wants me.

I swallow and process this knowledge as best I can. "What would you do in Portland?" I ask.

"I dunno. Get a job."

"It would be nice to have you around," I say. I reach out and tug at the pocket of his coat.

"It would be nice to be around," he says, moving closer.

I can't help myself, and in seconds we are all over each other. Making out, tearing at each other's clothes, breathing each other in in wild gasps. My brain starts to reel: tumbling forward into blissful blankness.

We end up inside my car. Stewart is mad with lust. So am I. I keep thinking we're going to stop. But I should know better.

And then it's happening. He's on top of me, crushing me in the backseat. I grab his hair, clutch at his shirt. I touch his face as it hovers over me.

And then as fast as it began, it's over and I'm blinking my eyes and he lifts himself off of me and we're sitting there, spent and half naked in the cold of my mom's Volvo.

Moments later, our clothes mostly back on, we sit together in a deep silence. "We probably shouldn't have done that," he says to me, a new seriousness in his voice.

"Don't say that," I murmur in the dark.

"But it isn't right."

"It's not perfect," I say. "Which is different than not right."

I take his hand. I kiss it. I hold it against my face.

"I love you, Stewart. And I always will."

"I love you too, Maddie. More than you'll ever know."

8

Two weeks later I have an anniversary of my own. On November 21, I have one year clean and sober.

I remember Cynthia telling me once: "There will be a point in your life when that day will be more sacred to you than your own birthday."

I don't know about that. But I am surprised I made it this long. I feel like I have to mark the occasion in some way.

So I go to the Young People's AA meeting that Trish and I went to. I don't know anyone, so I sit by myself waiting for the announcer person to ask if anyone is celebrating an anniversary. When he does, I raise my hand and say I am, I have one year. People burst into applause and I walk to the front to get my coin.

The people kinda go crazy. I don't know why. Maybe because I'm young and a girl. They whoop and clap and the street-kid skater boys, the ones Trish had crushes on, all high-five me as I make my way back to my chair.

Once I'm seated, I sit and hold the coin in my hand. The

coins they give you for thirty and sixty days are plastic, like poker chips. The one-year coin is brass. It's heavy in your hand. On one side it says: TO THINE OWN SELF BE TRUE. On the other side: ONE YEAR.

I grip it in my hand. One whole year.

For Thanksgiving my family drives up to Seattle to be with my mom's relatives, who are Irish and always get hammered during any holiday. This is apparently the gene pool I take after. I always liked the Reillys, but this year I am bored and I have to study and obviously I don't feel like playing football in the backyard with my drunk uncle Rob, who broke his wrist doing the exact same thing two years ago.

As Christmas approaches, whatever free time I have I spend with Martin and Grace and Doug Gerrard. The four of us go Christmas shopping one Saturday and Martin and I end up having a great talk at Starbucks about college and life and "what it all means" while Grace blows two hundred dollars on organic yoga mats for her sisters.

I also go shopping with Emily. With her I find a Christmas card for Stewart that shows these two teenagers in the 1950s making out in the back of a car. I also find him some cool motorcycle gloves and some thick wool socks that he'll need because it's cold in the basement where he's living. Then I find some flannel pajamas in a thrift store that have little elk heads on them. He'll like those. . . .

Emily notices the number of Stewart-related gifts and I'm forced to admit I'm kind of crushing on him again. I joke that as soon as Christmas is over, I am going to Centralia to claim what is rightfully mine.

At school, there's the usual holiday high jinks. Somebody puts mistletoe over the Senior Lounge doorway. Doug Gerrard and I actually walk right under it, to the wild giggling of several girls, but Doug is too scared to kiss me — even though I'm perfectly willing — and the whole thing becomes embarrassing.

Then there's the big holiday assembly in the gym. And the traditional singing of holiday carols in the hall. All of which is cheesy but I don't mind. I enjoy this stuff during my first sober holiday season. Last year at this time I was scrubbing toilets in a halfway house.

So it's all good to me.

The day before Christmas, I hang around the house getting ready for the Midnight Mass thing my parents go to on Christmas Eve. That's when Stewart calls. I think he's calling to wish me a Merry Christmas, but in fact, he has news: He is moving to Portland. For real. He's actually found a place for January. He's got enough money saved up to pay the deposit.

I'm stunned by this news. But I'm also happy. I have a huge smile on my face as he tells me. But I also don't know what this will mean. Is he doing this for me? Is this his attempt for us to finally be together? And if it is, could I do that? Would I want to?

Then I get my answer.

"There's another thing I wanted to tell you," he says, a strange quiet in his voice.

"What?" I ask him.

It takes him a minute to say it. "I've sorta been hanging out with someone."

"You have?" I say.

"Her name is Kirsten. You'll really like her. I met her down here. She wants to come to Portland too."

"Wait, so you're moving . . . with someone else?"

"No. Not right away. But just . . . it's something she's thinking about."

I'm sitting on our living room couch when he tells me this. I was heading upstairs to my room but now I am not going anywhere.

"So she's like . . . a girl . . . like a . . . girlfriend . . . ?"

"Well, I wouldn't exactly call it that."

"Does she think she is?"

"I don't know. . . ."

"So you guys are going out?"

"Kinda."

"Jeez, Stewart. I . . . I don't know what to say."

"I know. It's kinda weird."

"I mean, it's good," I say, my voice straining. "You need something . . . like that. . . ."

"I sorta thought you might be glad. Or actually, I wasn't sure what you would think. I never really know what you think."

"I am glad," I say, closing my eyes.

"Because you didn't seem like you wanted that . . . for us. . . ."

"What? What didn't I want?"

"You seemed like you wanted to focus on school and stuff. And not get tied down in a relationship."

He's right. That's what I wanted. *School and stuff.* What an idiotic thing to want.

"I've known her for a while," he says. "I was afraid to tell you. Because I didn't know if you'd be jealous or whatever."

"I . . . I guess I am jealous, a little. How can I not be? But I'm still . . . I'm still, you know . . . happy for you. . . ."

"I'm sorry if you're jealous."

"I'm not, though," I say, my voice starting to break. "I think it's great."

"You don't sound like it."

"I'll have to get used to it, Stewart. That's all."

"I'm sorry, Maddie. I didn't know how to tell you."

"Don't be sorry. God. Don't be sorry at all. I think it's great. I do. I think . . . it's great."

After I hang up, I look at my watch. I have to get ready for the Midnight Mass.

I walk up the stairs, and go to my room. I do my routine for when I have to get dressed up for things. I change my underwear and put on tights, and dig through my closet, considering my options.

My mom yells something to me from down the hall. I yell back, not saying anything, just like: "Yeah, okay!"

I find the gray wool skirt and red sweater-vest I wore sophomore year. I'm a little old for this outfit, but whatever. I slide the wool skirt on. My hands are shaking, I notice. I find the white blouse.

My mother yells again and this time I can't answer. I suddenly choke up. I can't speak. My eyes blur. And then there's no stopping the tears. They pour out of me. I drop the blouse and collapse, falling sideways into my closet, pulling coats and dresses down on top of myself.

I sit on the floor of my closet, half dressed, clothes and dresses hanging off my shoulders. And I cry and wail and sob.

Because it's finally happened. Completely. All the way.

I've lost Stewart. Just like I always knew I would.

10

At church, there are millions of people, millions of families. There are boys everywhere: nice boys, clean boys, polite boys. Boys from nice families. Boys with blazers and ties. Boys who smile at me and maybe would want to talk to me if we met somewhere else, at college, say, or at a nice party, or at somebody's nice house. I look at them with dead eyes. They are not my people. This is not my world.

Stewart is my person. Stewart is my world. He's been where I've been. He understands me in a way none of these people ever could, or ever will.

My parents and I kneel and stand and do the church things. We sing. And while other people sing, I start to cry again. My mom gives me Kleenex. Lots of boys stare at me then. They stare and look away.

spend New Year's Eve at Martin's house. We have a lame
party in his basement. It's me and Martin and Grace and
Doug Gerrard and Martin's little sister and two of her
eighth-grade friends. We watch the ball drop in Times Square
on TV and count down the seconds to the New Year. When
we reach exact midnight, Doug Gerrard, who has been waiting for this moment his whole life it seems, lamely attempts
to kiss me as Martin's little sister and her friends flash the
lights on and off with the light switch. I am willing to give
Doug a real kiss — poor guy — but he unexpectedly chickens
out at the last minute, so that our kiss becomes a peck, and
we end up standing two feet apart while Martin and Grace
go for the full-on New Year's Eve make-out session, dipping
each other and falling on the couch and giggling and having a
great time.

When I get home an hour later, I flip on the TV in the living
room and take off my coat.

A news reporter is on, one of the local guys. He's surrounded
by flashing police cars and ambulances, on a floodlit section of
Highway 211, not far from us.

"A terrible scene to have to report, Bill," says the reporter.

I glance up at the screen. Behind the reporter I see what's left of a green Toyota Highlander that looks vaguely familiar.

12

Ashley Brantley had been fighting with her friend Jayna Rosenfeld all day. (This is Bryce Handler's version of the story.) The problem was Jayna's favorite hoodie, which Ashley had borrowed and kept for over a month and which Jayna made her swear she'd give back in time for the big New Year's party at Courtney Robbins's house. Naturally, Ashley forgot. So that afternoon, Jayna drove over to Ashley's and actually walked into her house and into her room and into her closet and took it back. She did this while Ashley was standing right there, talking to Bryce on the phone.

Ashley followed Jayna out of the house (while still on the phone with Bryce) and accused Jayna of stealing Jayna's own hoodie. Jayna accused Ashley of being a stupid bitch. Other, similar insults were exchanged. The battle was on.

Later, when they were both at Courtney Robbins's New Year's party, Rachel, who was Ashley's newest friend, was sent by Ashley to tell Jayna she was still a stupid bitch, and also a liar, a thief, and a skank, and that their friendship was over. Rachel was probably thrilled to deliver this news. Rachel had been scheming all along to replace Jayna as Ashley's best friend.

Ashley and Jayna avoided each other until after midnight. They finally met in the driveway, where they yelled, screamed, and called each other stupid bitches for over an hour as a fairly large group of partygoers looked on.

Then Jayna tried to leave. She got in her forest green Toyota Highlander and started the engine, but Ashley opened the door and pulled her out by her hair. Jayna then punched Ashley in the head and Ashley kicked Jayna in the knee.

After more kicking, punching, and hair-pulling, Ashley outmaneuvered Jayna and ended up in the idling Highlander, in the driver's seat. Rachel, not wanting to be separated from her new best friend, jumped into the passenger side. Ashley slammed her door shut, and threatened to drive away. Jayna jerked open the back door (it was her car, after all), jumped in, and tried to lunge through the seats and grab the car keys out of the ignition. Rachel, who was closer, also had a chance to grab the keys but was afraid to enter into this epic battle of the two most popular girls in her class.

Ashley fought off Jayna and, to further establish her own dominance over the situation, shifted the car into drive and slammed down the accelerator. The car shot onto the street, shutting all the open doors and violently throwing all three girls back in their seats. Ashley, who had almost no experience driving, then regained control of the car and took off down the road. Within seconds, they were going forty miles an hour. Jayna, who was used to Ashley's reckless theatrics, screamed at the top of her lungs for Ashley to stop the car now!

She didn't.

Nobody knows for sure what happened next. People in the driveway watched the car swerve wildly from side to side. They watched it run the stop sign at Highway 211, and rip a tire-burning right turn, and accelerate. Probably, by that point, Jayna was afraid to do anything. They were going too fast to grab the wheel. They were now at the mercy of Ashley.

Rachel, for her part, was most likely unafraid. In her mind, nothing bad could happen to Ashley Brantley. She was too perfect, too beautiful, too charmed. It was like the high school gods had blessed her with every imaginable advantage. She was indestructible.

But in fact, she was not. Neither were the D'Augustinos, an elderly couple, who were driving home from a small gathering at their son's house. They were driving slowly, cautiously. They knew what night it was.

Ashley hit the D'Augustinos head-on at seventy-three miles an hour, killing herself and the defenseless D'Augustinos instantly. In that way, maybe Ashley was blessed. She never had to think about what she had done.

Jayna, in the backseat, was not so lucky. Though crushed and mangled, she did manage to gasp for air for almost a half hour before the arriving paramedics lost her pulse amid the wreckage of the destroyed Toyota Highlander.

Rachel fared the worst. She was crushed too, pinned, her young face sliced in half by a piece of jagged plastic. She lived, though, and made it to the hospital, surviving four emergency surgeries before she too slipped away despite the best efforts of the doctors, who couldn't repair her hemorrhaging organs or splintered limbs quickly enough. You had to wonder what her last thoughts were, if she had a chance to reflect on her parents' warning two weeks before, that they had heard bad things about "that Brantley girl."

13

The three funerals occur on three successive days.

The turnout for all three is overwelming. Hundreds of people come. People from school. People from the area. Mr. Brown is at every one. I see him in the back, setting up extra folding chairs.

There are articles in the newspaper all week and hours of coverage on TV. "The New Year's Tragedy," it's called. Because the girls were young and pretty, there are pictures of them everywhere: the three sparkling teenagers, their hopes, their dreams, their perfect suburban lives, all of it tragically cut short.

There are also articles about teenage drinking, teenage alcoholism, should we make teenagers wait until they're eighteen to drive? Which is funny, considering Ashley was fifteen and didn't even have a learner's permit.

I go early to Ashley's service to see if Emily needs anything, but she sticks close to her family. Even when I circle through the crowd to talk to her, she shies away. She doesn't seem to want any help.

So I stand with Martin and Grace and Doug Gerrard. Grace keeps saying, "It's so awful." When Martin and I are alone for a moment, he looks at me and jokes, "Wasn't our first date a funeral?"

It's not very funny, but I smile, so he won't feel bad.

It's a hard three days. Nobody knows how to act. Nobody knows what to say.

Grace won't shut up with her "It's so awful."

After the last service, for Jayna, everyone goes to a huge reception at our school's gymnasium. More than two thousand people show up. The community needs this final ritual. The school needs it. The parents need it.

But not me. I go home. I've had enough.

part six

On February 1, Stewart moves into his new apartment in Portland. He calls to tell me. He wants me to come down and see it and help him unpack. I don't know if that's the best idea, but in the end I can't say no.

I show up at noon on a Saturday. The building is not so nice. And it's in a bad part of town. I park and hike up the stairs. I knock on the door of apartment 305. The door is ajar and I slowly push it open.

The apartment is tiny, for starters. It's also dirty and falling apart. Paint is peeling from one of the walls. One of the windows is cracked.

"Hey!" says Stewart, appearing from behind a closet door. "What do you think?"

"Wow. I . . . uh . . . it's very . . ."

"I know, I know, but it's dirt cheap," he tells me, putting a box on the floor.

I take a few tentative steps inside. "The floor is uneven," I say. "You're going to get splinters."

"I like to think it has *personality*."

"There's air blowing through. I can feel it."

"It's February. It'll warm up in a couple months."

I look out the window. "Is it safe here?"

"Probably not," he says. "But it's not like I have anything to steal."

There's no furniture, no place to sit. I help Stewart scoot some of his boxes around.

"You don't have much stuff," I say.

"I don't believe in material possessions," he jokes.

"It's a good thing."

"You want a cup of tea?"

I do. Stewart finds a pot in one of the boxes and fills it with water. I watch him do this. He looks different: older, healthier. And then I realize the biggest difference. His hair is short and it's not dyed. It's a very ordinary brown.

We drink our tea. I sit on one of the boxes with my cup. "So where's Kirsten?" I ask. Kirsten, it turns out, is moving in immediately.

"She's getting us a bed. From her mom's house."

I nod.

Stewart nods too.

"How's it going with her?" I ask.

"Good," he says. "She's psyched to move in."

"Was it her idea . . . to move in?"

"We kinda had to. She had to sign the lease."

"Oh."

"I think it'll be okay." He bends over a box and pulls out some cruddy dishes. "I know it's weird, you and her. But I think you're gonna like her. She has a good heart."

"Yeah . . ." I say, my voice trailing off. I look around at the cold, dirty, crappy apartment. "I wish you luck. Living with someone."

Stewart frowns. "You say that like you and I will never hang out. We totally will."

"And Kirsten will be cool with that?"

Stewart shrugs. "Why wouldn't she be?"

"Because we had sex? Because we were together?"

"Yeah, I guess."

"She does know about that, doesn't she?"

"Yeah, of course. But I also told her, you know, that you and I . . ."

"You and I what?"

"That we're important to each other in other ways. Beyond that. We went through rehab together. We have that bond. . . ."

I drink my tea.

"I *hope* we have that bond," he continues. "I hope we'll still be friends."

"I hate that phrase, *being friends*."

"Well, yeah, but our situation is sort of different. Right? We're like comrades. We've been through the wars together."

I don't answer. But he's right. I don't want to admit it. But he's right.

2

Meanwhile, back at school, I have a new friendship problem: Emily Brantley. Of course, I'm super nice, once we're back in school. Also, I give her space, to let her decide when she wants to start hanging out, or doing normal things or whatever. I don't freak out when she seems to avoid me the first couple days back at school. But then I notice she's hanging out with other people. She's going back to her old friends. And she's still avoiding me.

A week later, I hear that she visited UCLA, which is her first choice for colleges. But when I go to her locker after school one day, she can't look me in the eye.

"So how was UCLA?" I ask her.

"It was okay. You know. Fun in the sun." She's still not looking at me.

"Do you still want to go there?" I ask.

"I dunno, maybe."

I watch her yank a book out from the bottom of her locker. "What's up, Emily?" I ask.

"Nothing," she says.

"It seems like you don't want to talk to me."

She shakes her head. "It's not that. It's just that I always think of Ashley when I see you."

"Yeah. It's weird."

"I don't blame you or anything. It's not like that."

"I know."

"Your name always comes up, though. At the grief counselor's. She says I feel guilty because I wanted you to help her, instead of doing it myself."

"You can't think about stuff like that," I say calmly. "Whose fault it was . . . or who could have stopped it. Nobody could have stopped it."

"That's what everybody says."

"That night I talked to her. She was barely listening."

Emily looks at the ground. "Maybe you didn't say it right."

I'm a little surprised by this statement. "What?" I say.

"I just mean, maybe you could have explained it better," Emily says. "She looked up to you. You were the one person who could have influenced her."

"But I couldn't. That's what I'm saying. Nobody could have."

"I know," says Emily. "I'm sorry. I just have to let it go."

"You do. You really do."

"Well," she says. "Hopefully I'll be in California next year. And everything will be better then."

"I hope we can be friends again, Emily," I say.

"Yeah," she says. "Some things just aren't possible, I guess."

She shuts her locker as she says this. I stand there, speechless, while she turns and walks away.

3

That's how it goes during February. The weather sucks. People are on edge. Everyone feels awful. The whole school seems to be under a dark cloud.

It gets so bad, Mr. Brown has another assembly where a grief specialist addresses the school. He says nice things about Ashley, Jayna, and Rachel, but what he really wants is for us to get on with our lives, enjoy the rest of the school year, let go.

People do their best.

Then Emily stops coming to school, and there are rumors that she's in the hospital after a prescription drug overdose, though when she returns to school, the story changes to she had the flu.

I have my own moments of dark thoughts. I wonder if Emily was right. Maybe I could have talked to Ashley differently, been more serious with her. I want to talk to Stewart about it but when I call him, he's eating dinner with Kirsten, and it's totally awkward and I quickly hang up.

One interesting thing that happens: My obsession to go to college back east suddenly disappears. I wake up one morning and I couldn't care less. I want to stay in Portland. I want to get a job. I want to do something simple and obvious, become a dog walker or work at an arts supply store.

The last thing I want is more school, more pressure, more stress.

It's too late, though. My applications are in, and a month later I get accepted to the University of Massachusetts. It's not even that great of a school. And my parents will have to pay out-of-state tuition, which means it's gonna cost a small fortune.

When I get the acceptance letter, I can't remember why I even applied there. It doesn't make any sense.

Fortunately, my parents understand my mood swings. They tell me not to worry about it. "Just go," says my dad, who knows about such things. "Just see what it's like. If you hate it, come back."

So I fill out the forms and send in the packet. My dad sends a check.

Then it's done. Mad Dog Maddie is officially going to college.

t's early April when I finally meet Kirsten.

Everyone involved is anxious about this moment, but it happens naturally enough, when Stewart has his seven-month anniversary.

We meet at that same Young People's AA meeting, which Stewart goes to now that he lives in Portland. I walk in and see Stewart and Kirsten sitting in the middle row of folding chairs. Kirsten looks nervous, but Stewart is his usual happy, goofy self — until he sees me coming over to say hi.

Kirsten stands up when she realizes who I am.

She is thin and wispy and has an eyebrow ring that is too big for her face. She's dressed in a kind of alternative-vegan-punk style. The main thought I have when I see her is: *small town*.

She is a very sincere person, I see that right away. I can also tell she's afraid of me. I try to be nice. I hug her and find she is even thinner than she looks and she smells vaguely like a health food store. It's hard to tell if she's actually pretty, but she is definitely devoted to Stewart. Maybe that's what he needed all along: less smart, more heart.

I sit next to them, which feels uncomfortable, but I do it anyway. The AA meeting begins and they make the announcements and then give out the coins. Stewart, as usual, is very popular among the other AA boys and girls. When it's his turn to get his coin, the place erupts in cheers and hilarity. Someone hits him in the back of the head with a knit cap. Someone else yells out: "Aye, Stewaht, ya drunken bah-stad!"

He takes his coin, squeezes it in his fist, holds it over his head in victory as everyone claps and whistles.

I glance over at Kirsten, who seems a little unnerved. Maybe she's never been to one of these. She probably wasn't expecting it to be a basement full of skateboard hooligans.

After the meeting, a bunch of the guys take Stewart down the street to the local coffee place. Kirsten and I follow along and sit quietly while the boys tease and harass Stewart.

We drink our coffees and I finally ask Kirsten if she has a job in Portland yet. She says she's selling flowers at a shop downtown. I know the place — there's always willowy hippie chicks working there. It seems perfect.

She asks me if I have a job, and I say no, I'm a senior in high school.

She didn't know this. She thought I was older. She looks at Stewart like, why didn't he tell her?

That's how it goes. Weird. Awkward. But Kirsten is nice. She means well. She isn't going to hurt him in any way.

But I worry about Stewart. Still. I don't know why exactly.

Even with his AA crew and his seven months sober and his loving girlfriend and his brand-new job cleaning carpets in office buildings.

Still, I worry.

5

thought I might find you here," says Martin one day, when he finds me in the library at lunch.

"What? I can still come here," I say.

"You're back in *hide-out* mode again," he says.

"No, I'm not," I say.

"That's okay. I am too. At this point."

"Where's Grace?"

"She just found out Tara Peterson is also going to Mount Holyoke, so now the two of them are best friends."

"Tara Peterson? Is going to Mount Holyoke? I'd kill to go to Mount Holyoke!"

"Yeah. I guess all those club activities paid off."

"The world is so unfair," I say. I go back to my crossword puzzle.

Martin takes a seat, and since he's already accepted at Stanford and therefore does no homework — he doesn't even have his backpack — he just sits there. "Being a senior is such a classic letdown," he says, leaning back in his chair. "All this buildup and anticipation. And then you get here and it's nothing. You're just killing time."

"Welcome to my world," I say.

He stares at my crossword puzzle. "You wanna do something this weekend?" he asks me.

"What happened to Grace?"

"She's going to Seattle."

"Oh."

"We could go ice-skating."

"Okay. Whatever."

He lets his chair fall back down with a thud. "I think Grace is going to dump me," he says.

"Why do you think that?"

"She likes this other guy. Frank Perrone. He goes to Bradley Day School."

"When did that happen?"

"Her mother's been trying to fix them up since seventh grade. Her mother's not into me. She likes tall, handsome, athletic guys. Not computer geeks."

"And Grace is going along with it?"

"It seems like she is. She keeps talking about how long-distance relationships don't work. And how we're going to be on different coasts."

"That's not good."

"I know. She's so logical. It creeps me out. Boys are supposed to be logical. Not girls."

Martin and I go ice-skating that weekend and, on Monday, Grace breaks up with him, blaming it partially on me, telling everyone that Martin secretly liked me all along.

This pisses me off, and I consider going to her locker and punching her face in. But then I doubt that I would be able to summon up my Mad Dog Maddie persona long enough to pull it off. Probably she would stand up to me in her prissy way and I'd be the one humiliated.

So I do nothing, because who cares anyway?

Martin is so right about senior year. It is a study in irrelevancy. Unless you really love playing Frisbee, or finally getting to be president of Citizenship Club.

In the end, it's all for the best, because without Grace around, Martin and I can hang out as much as we want, which is pretty much all we do during the last months of school. We hang out and walk around and lie in the grass above the baseball diamond. We chew on grass, look at the clouds. It's fun, but also bittersweet. So much has happened to me in the last four years.

Who knew I would be sad to leave Evergreen High School?

6

A t graduation, I get stuck standing next to Jake and Alex, of all people. I assume they've never forgiven me for breaking our stoner bond. But I'm wrong about that. They're super nice, especially Alex, who suddenly wants to know what I'm doing over the summer and asks me out in a vague, noncommittal way.

Afterward, I hang out with Martin, whose whole family has shown up. Martin's parents love me now. Then Grace comes over and freaks out when Martin won't take a picture with her. "But you were my senior boyfriend!" she insists. Grace's mother even comes over and gets involved.

Martin still refuses. He won't discuss it. No picture. And that's that. I stay out of it, but secretly I'm cheering him on.

I can't wait to see what happens to Martin, going off to Stanford, and then on to the rest of his life.

He's gonna kick ass. That's what I predict. He's gonna be president or cure cancer or something.

I mean it. I'm totally serious.

part seven

1

And then I drink.

It happens this way: It's the middle of summer and Emily's friend Paul blows into town. He's looking for Emily but she's on vacation, so I meet him and we end up at a party Paul knows about, at a house of Reed College students. There's a lot of booze and stuff around, but I'm not uncomfortable. I don't feel particularly vulnerable or anything. It's just another night of hanging out.

Then, at one point, I'm standing with some people listening to a funny story and this guy comes over and he's gripping four longneck beers in one hand and he's about to drop them. So everyone reaches out and grabs one and I do too, being helpful, and this being a Reed College house, and it seeming like the collegiate thing to do. But the guy next to me, when he takes his, he lifts it straight up to his mouth and takes a long swig. Another guy, across from me, does the exact same thing, and so I do too, like in perfect unison, all of us do, like fish all turning at the same moment, or birds all taking off at the same time.

At first, I'm just going to take a sip, not even a sip, a fake, tiny non-sip, for appearance's sake. I do this because I'm having fun and I like these people and it's summer and because I feel like it. But when I lift the bottle to my mouth, I change my mind and actually let some of the beer go into my mouth. I remember the taste so well, it's so familiar, it seems perfectly natural to drink more, to take a real sip, since I never do anymore. It stings a little and my chest burns for a moment and when I lower the bottle, I burp, and everyone looks at me strangely, and the guy who was telling the funny story says: "Looks like we got a party girl here!" I stare at him blankly and put the bottle back in my mouth and take another solid swig. Then, just for the hell of it, I drain the rest of the bottle. I burp again.

Everyone thinks this is funny for some reason. I'm not sure why. I also don't care. I reach over and take the beer that the guy on my right is holding (saying "gimme that" for comic effect) and drink half of it and hand it back to him and they all laugh and think this is hilarious as well, though again, I'm not sure why. What's so funny about drinking beer?

I turn and walk away and then I realize that I have drunk alcohol and that I don't do that anymore, I can't do it, I'm forbidden from ever doing it, but I don't care, and I see a plastic cup, half full of red wine, and I pick it up and drink some on my way toward the front porch, where I'm thinking Paul might be. I don't know where he went. He probably found some girl. *That isn't cool*, I think. *Why did he leave me alone here? At a party where I don't know anyone?* I decide then and there: *This is all Paul's fault.*

I find myself sitting on the steps outside and that's when it hits me. *I drank.* I feel sick to my stomach but I also feel light-headed and relaxed and it's good, the feeling, even though there's a falseness to it. I feel warm and good and insulated from things and happy and comfortable, and I have this feeling that I don't want to waste this, I want to do something fun, something like *drink more*, because really I'm only half drunk, I'm *almost* drunk, that's no fun, and if everyone's going to be pissed at me anyway, I might as well go all the way, I might as well get my money's worth.

I drink my wine. I wish I had a cigarette or something to do with my hands, though I don't smoke, never have, except a couple times when I was trashed. Maybe someone has pot, though. That would be fun. I finish the wine and go back inside.

I look for weed; I smelled some earlier, but nobody's smoking any now. I go into the kitchen and find another beer in the fridge. I twist open the top. I forgot what that's like, how the little metal edges cut into your palm as you twist it. I put the bottle to my mouth and drink it, without rushing this time, tasting it, letting it pour into my mouth and over my tongue and down my throat. I love it, I love the taste of it, the smell of it. I savor every drop, then I lower it and burp and someone is there, saying something to me.

I don't hear them. That's the other thing that happens: I become instantly hard. I become hard as steel; nobody's going to tell me anything. No useless chitchat for Mad Dog Maddie. I instantly have no tolerance for any of the happy party bullshit going on around me. Stupid Reedies. And where the fuck is Paul?

Then I think: *Jack Daniel's*. That's what I really want. I start digging through the bottles of liquor scattered around the kitchen, I paw through the cupboards, I go into the other room where the drink table is. There's no Jack Daniel's, only Bacardi rum, so I pour some of that into a glass with some flat Pepsi and drink it down and pour a little more rum in it and now I am getting there. Now I am where I want to be. But then, of course, a moment later, that feeling fades. I'm not *quite* there. I need more.

A half hour later, I am drunk. Deeply, solidly, falling-down drunk. Somehow, I get myself out of the house. I wobble onto the front porch, down the steps, and then, without planning to, I find myself walking down the middle of the street.

The night sky is glassy and strange above me. Nothing is real. I bend over and puke on somebody's lawn, holding my hair back and then continuing on, like everything is perfectly normal.

"*Stew-art,*" I sing out, releasing the word upward and letting it drift away from me like a cloud of breath on a winter day.

I let my eyes rest on the night sky above me. It glows an orangish yellow from the city light, but strangely so, and I notice everything is off-kilter slightly and not quite in focus. My feet trip over the curb, and someone seems to slug me, but no, it's the ground, I fell, I'm in the grass again, on my side. I try to get up and I'm all over the place. I stumble into a parked car. I stop then, holding the side mirror, smiling to myself at the absurdity of it all.

"*Stew-art . . .*" I sing.

2

everal hours later I manage to call Stewart, not to be rescued, more because it's funny, and I'm getting him back and also because I'm on an unfamiliar street somewhere, and some creepy guy is watching me from the entrance of a convenience store.

I have no clue where I am. I sit on a curb in front of a pizza place. I have puked again and now sit stunned, stupid, wanting more alcohol but also knowing that it's over, whatever it was, this storm that blew in from the east, or wherever storms blow in from, and I'm just sad now and crying and drunk and useless like I always was, like I always will be. Someone should shoot me in the head for all the good I do people. . . . Ashley . . . I let her die. . . . Trish, I couldn't be bothered to help her. . . . Even Stewart I couldn't stick with, even though I loved him more than anything in the world. . . .

Stew-art . . .

S tewart appears across the street. I see him getting out of an old Ford Fiesta, which must be Kirsten's. When I see him crossing the street, I start to cry.

He sits down with me on the curb.

"Well, look at you," he says, putting his arm around me.

I start to cry more and he puts his other arm around me and I bury myself in his sweaty armpit. The smell of him is home to me. The smell of him is safety and understanding and love to me.

"It's okay, Maddie," Stewart whispers to me. "It happens. . . ."

I cry into his chest. I cry and cry and cry. There's a whole lot of stuff in there that needs to come out. And it does.

4

wake up the next morning and I'm in a bed. I don't know where I am and I sit up and look around and I am in Stewart and Kirsten's dirty apartment. I'm in their bed, in my panties and T-shirt.

Stewart is gone. Kirsten is sitting on the couch with a blanket over her; that's where she spent the night. I see an army surplus sleeping bag on the floor, which is where Stewart must have slept.

My first thought is: *Why didn't they take me home? My parents are going to kill me.*

"Hey," Kirsten says to me in her timid voice.

"Where's Stewart?" I say back. That's when I feel the dull pain begin to invade my brain. My mouth too; it's dry and sticky and parched.

"He went to get coffee."

"Did anybody call my parents?" I ask.

Kirsten nods. "Stewart did."

That's a relief. I look around. My head is beginning to throb.

"Don't you have coffee here?" I say, gazing blankly in the direction of the tiny kitchen area.

"He wanted to get something from Starbucks. He said you liked fancy coffee."

"Oh," I say.

She smiles politely at me from across the room. She is meek, odd, a mouse of a girl.

"Well, thanks for . . . letting me crash . . ." I say, looking around at the one-room apartment that is their home.

Kirsten remains where she is. This must not be fun for her. The old flame crashing at the house. Does she know that Stewart and I still love each other? She must.

The door opens. Stewart comes in. He's got three Starbucks coffees stacked one on top of the other.

He gives one to me, one to Kirsten, takes one himself. He sits on the floor Indian style and takes a sip of it.

"Don't you guys have a table or anything?" I say.

They don't.

"I called your parents," says Stewart.

"What did they say?"

"Nothing. I told them you had to sleep over."

"Did you tell them I was drunk?"

"I told them you fell asleep. They seemed kind of worried, though."

At that moment my phone rings. Stewart has it in his pocket and he hands it to me. It's my mom.

"Hey, Mom," I say.

"Honey! Thank God. Where are you? What happened? Paul called here last night and said he lost you."

"Yeah. We got separated at that party."

"And then Stewart called and said you weren't feeling well."

"I know. I got drunk."

"You what?"

"I drank. I got drunk. I just . . . drank for some reason. Stewart came and got me."

"Oh, Maddie! That's terrible. Where are you now?"

"Stewart's."

"Your father and I will come get you. Don't go anywhere. What's the address there?"

"I'm fine, Mom. I'm just sitting here. This is probably the best place for me right now."

"We'll come get you."

"Stewart is sober, Mom. He's here. I'm fine. I'll be home in an hour."

"Honey, please, let us come get you."

"No, Mom. Stewart can give me a ride home. Don't do anything. I'm perfectly safe."

"Oh, Madeline! Don't drink any more. We can send you back to Spring Meadow. I'll call Dr. Bernstein!"

"Mother, stop it! I'm fine. I'll be home in an hour."

"Why the hell were you by yourself, at a college party, in the first place?" Stewart says to me as we leave his building. Kirsten walks with us, though she hangs back slightly to let us talk.

"It was just a party," I say. "There wasn't anything wrong with it. I'm going to college in six weeks. I can't *not* go to parties."

We drive across town to my neighborhood. We don't talk for a while. It's a hot summer morning and Kirsten opens her window and lets the air blow through the backseat.

Stewart is pissed. He keeps starting to talk, then doesn't. Finally, he clears his throat. "You know what you gotta do now, right?" he says to me.

"No, what?"

"You gotta go to AA."

I say nothing. I've never been a big fan of AA.

"I know you think it's lame or whatever," says Stewart.

"I never said that."

"But you gotta go. And you gotta do all the crap they say. Make friends, get a sponsor, volunteer for stuff. Go to Sober Bowling."

"Sober *Bowling*? Are you serious?"

"Hey, you weren't too stuck-up for movie night."

"Actually, I was. I went to movie night as a protest."

"Then go to Sober Bowling as a protest. Do it *all* as a protest. It doesn't matter. You have to go. Every day. Twice a day."

"I can't do that."

He looks over at me. "If you don't, you're gonna lose everything. And you've got stuff to lose."

"No, I don't," I say.

He says nothing back but he knows he's right. I know he's right too.

5

My parents, naturally, are out of their minds with worry. They come running out of the house when we pull up. My mom hugs me and my dad is right behind her, on his cell phone, trying to reach Cynthia, my old counselor. It turns out she doesn't work at Spring Meadow anymore.

We all go inside. Stewart and I try to explain to them that I don't need to go back to Spring Meadow.

"It's just a slip," I tell my parents.

They don't know what that is.

"It means I had a momentary lapse, but I'm not gonna go crazy. I need to go to AA meetings."

"But you've already been to those."

"I'm gonna go like . . . all the time," I say grumpily. "That's what I was supposed to be doing from the start."

This is news to my parents.

Everyone kind of calms down after that. My parents can see that I haven't turned into a zombie. I haven't lost my mind.

One fun thing: watching my parents fall all over themselves thanking Stewart. Dad shaking his hand. Mom hugging him with all her heart. Mr. High School Dropout Motorcycle Boy saved their precious daughter. That makes the whole thing worth it. Sort of.

Stewart and Kirsten have to go. I give them both hugs and promise to call. They walk back to Kirsten's Ford Fiesta and my mom shuts the door.

But then, as I'm going upstairs, the doorbell rings.

I go answer it and it's Kirsten. I left my phone in their car. "You forgot this."

I take it from her. "Thanks," I say. "And thanks for letting me stay with you guys last night."

"Sure," she says. She hesitates a moment. "And there's something else," she says.

"Yes?"

This is hard for her. But she gets it out: "Stewart said you . . . saved his life once. In Redland. And I wanted to thank you for that."

I stare at her. "I didn't save his life. I dragged him home. Like he did for me last night."

"He said it might have cost you your chance to go to college."

"I'm still going to college. Don't worry about me."

She gets a little embarrassed then. "I wanted to . . . thank you. For whatever you did to help Stewart. I love him so much. And he's helped me in so many ways."

This is a little too much information for me. But I try to be nice.

"I'm glad you guys are together," I say. "I think you make him very happy." I don't even know if I mean this, but I say it anyway.

Her whole face lights up. She takes my hand and squeezes it and then does this little-girl run back to the Ford Fiesta, which Stewart revs impatiently.

I walk up the stairs to my room and start looking up AA meetings on my computer.

So then, after already completing The Most Boring Summer Ever at community college, I begin my Even More Boring Summer Ever of going to endless AA meetings.

I go every day. I go to a lunchtime meeting. Then I sit around by myself at the coffee place and go again to the afternoon meeting.

I go early. I introduce myself to people. I sweep the floors and help stack the chairs. I get to know people. I get to know Claire, who makes pottery and does yoga every morning at 5:00 a.m. I meet Missy, who is a cashier at Safeway and has female baldness issues. I meet Brooke, who is eighteen and lives on the street because her parents burned down their trailer when their meth lab blew up.

Oh, the fun, the fun.

I also meet Susan. She's a housewife. She wants to be my sponsor. So then I have to hang out with her and call her all the time.

The whole thing is a royal pain in the ass. But whatever. I just do it. Why not? What else do I have to do?

• • •

The one fun thing is the Young People's meeting. This is the same one Trish went to and Stewart still goes to occasionally. Now I go every Monday night at 7:00.

It's hilarious. Everyone goofs around and says outrageous things. There's a gang of cute skateboarder guys who are always getting in trouble and showing up with black eyes from street fights and stuff.

They're like Jake and Raj and Alex, except they've actually done the stuff those guys dream about. They hop trains to California, they skateboard everywhere, they live in an old squat house in the industrial district. They are some serious badass boys.

Of course I totally want to hang out with them. I meet this girl Antoinette who is friends with them, and she and I hang out a little. She's a chain-smoking, multi-pierced, train-wreck type. But we hit it off.

Anyway, the skater boys barely notice me until one night we're all standing around in the parking lot and for some reason I mention Stewart. They all know Stewart; he's sort of their idol, so that's big points for me. So then I jokingly say I was sort of in love with him and they all laugh and say every girl is in love with Stewart, and then I consider saying something else, like, no, I was *really* in love with him, we were *together*, but that doesn't seem wise and I shut up, and then they invite me and Antoinette to go skating with them. We end up wandering all over the city until four in the morning, and it turns into the best night of my whole summer.

After that, Monday night becomes what I wait for all week.

But by then, summer's almost over.

part eight

At the end of August, I begin packing and buying toiletries and getting ready to leave for the University of Massachusetts. It's a weird place to tell people you're going. It doesn't exactly roll off your tongue.

On my last packing day, my mom surprises me with a cheesy hoodie that says UMASS on the front. It comes via FedEx. I guess she hasn't noticed I'm not exactly a school-spirit type. I pretend to pack it anyway, and then, when she's not looking, I stuff it behind some old T-shirts in my closet.

On the big day, my parents take me to the airport and I watch out the window as we drive beside the long, manicured strip of grass. It makes you think, driving to the airport. It makes you wonder where you'll go in life.

Inside the terminal I see other young people going to college. Many of them wear school names on their hoodies. I see one for Boston College, one for University of Washington, one for Arizona State.

"See? You should have worn your sweatshirt on the plane!" says my mother.

We arrive at the security checkpoint and my parents get weepy. They are happy for me, but also, deep in their hearts, probably terrified. They don't know the police department in Massachusetts. They don't know the sheriff's office. They don't know the number of the detox places, or the psych wards, or the names of any good doctors.

Who will they call if I don't come home at night? How will they even know if I come home at all?

They are taking a big chance on this. We all are.

2

T en hours later, I'm there, on campus, jet-lagged, bleary-eyed, wheeling my suitcase through the strange and sticky East Coast air.

UMass is a huge state school surrounded by a cluster of smaller elite colleges. That's why I came here: because there's an exchange program between these schools. If you go to UMass, you can also take classes at Smith and Amherst and get a taste of the academic big leagues.

I register and find my dorm. I meet my suite mates. Living with other people was my parents' idea, for my own safety. My suite mates are two girls from Boston. They're not what you'd call studious, and are mostly interested in boys and celebrities and reality TV shows. They get totally smashed every Thursday, Friday, Saturday, and usually Sunday night, mostly at fraternity parties but also with old high school friends or oily-faced guys in Celtics jerseys, who show up in tricked-out Honda Civics.

I resolve to make the best of it, and once I've got my bearings I begin working the system. I go to the Dean of Students office, and after a couple dead ends, I find a woman named

Marianne, who I sit with for an hour and spill out my whole story.

She totally understands and helps me strategize. She thinks I might be able to transfer if I really bust my ass in my first year. In the meantime she gets me special permission forms so I can take classes at the other schools.

The one class I really want to take is at Smith College. It's a whole class just about Sylvia Plath. Plus, the professor, Sarah L. Slotnik, wrote a famous book about her that was an international bestseller.

Marianne totally helps me and figures out how to get me enrolled in this class spring semester. I'm so psyched. There's just one small thing I have to do: Go find Professor Slotnik and get her permission to take the class.

3

I haven't even been on the Smith campus yet when I set out to find Professor Slotnik. I take the shuttle bus that drives around to the different colleges.

I get off at Smith. I'm totally lost at first, but that's okay, I have a half hour before Professor Slotnik's office hours begin, so I walk around.

Smith is very posh, very elegant. The buildings are old and freshly painted and have real ivy on them, just like the pictures. There are walking paths, perfectly groomed, that weave through little stone courtyards and down to a lake at the bottom of the hill.

And the Smith girls: There is no mistaking them for the UMass girls. They seem to glow with intelligence and sophistication. They look like they've lived in Paris and Peru and all over the world. For them, going to Smith is not a dream come true; it's a natural stop. It's where they belong.

I check the books they carry under their arms. I look at what shoes they wear. I listen to how they talk. I swear to God, I've never felt like such an alien. I feel weirder here than I did at Spring Meadow.

But then I gather myself. I gotta meet with Professor Slotnik. I'm a little scared now, having seen the other Smith students. But I can do it. I feel pretty sure of myself.

I walk into the English Department. A woman at a desk tells me that Professor Slotnik will see me as soon as she can. I take a seat on a polished chair that is probably made of pure mahogany. The whole English Department looks like something out of *Masterpiece Theater*. Everything is dusted and vacuumed, and even the metal windowpanes shine like they've been polished by servants.

It's all a little unnerving, but I try to use my fear to my advantage. I try to see myself as the underdog, the spunky outsider with a heart of gold who, if you give her a chance, will work her fingers to the bone.

Finally, the woman at the desk gestures to me that it's my turn. I step cautiously to the door. I peek in. Professor Slotnik sits reading at her desk.

"Yes?" she says, looking up. "Can I help you?"

I open my mouth to speak but then nothing comes out. It's because Professor Slotnik looks like a movie star. No, she looks *better* than a movie star. She has radiant blue eyes, full lips, strangely ageless skin. Her stylishly coifed hair is completely white but it doesn't make her look old. It makes her look *sexy*.

"Yes?" she says with queenly reserve.

I start again. "Uh . . . yes. I just wanted . . . to ask you . . ."

"Please, come in." She gestures at the chair across from her desk.

I come in. I sit. I try to gather my thoughts. But I can't think of how to talk to her.

"What is it?" she asks me.

"I . . . uh . . . I want to take your course? The Sylvia Plath course?"

Sarah L. Slotnik stares at me. Her face is so perfectly formed, I feel unworthy to gaze upon it.

"And you're a student here at Smith?"

"Uh . . . no. I'm at . . . UMass."

"UMass?" she says, letting her surprise show. "Well, as you can understand, the course is for Smith students. They get first priority."

"I know, but the thing is . . . I mean . . . that's what —"

"If we had extra spots available, which we don't, the Smith students on the waiting list would be first."

"No, I know —" I say.

"All twenty spaces are taken," she says, a strain in her voice, since I am now wasting her time. "And considering the waiting list is over a hundred names long, there's absolutely nothing I can do."

"But if I wanted to take it next year?" I stammer. "Could I sign up now?"

"Next year I will be on sabbatical in Vienna."

But I read Sylvia Plath in rehab, I want to say. *I've had a rough time. I'm different, I'm interesting, I've suffered!*

"Now, if there's nothing else," she says, a growing coldness in her voice. "I need to finish here."

"No . . . there's nothing else."

I get up and nearly walk into the wall on my way out. I lurch down the stairs and out the front of the building.

I was going to have lunch in the Smith student center but I decide against that. I go straight back to the shuttle bus stop and collapse on the bench.

• • •

When I get back to UMass, my suite mates are painting their toenails and watching *Judge Judy*.

Though it's 3:30 in the afternoon, I get in my bed and pull my covers over me and turn and face the wall.

Then I notice my phone is beeping in my pack. It's probably my parents; I told them about my "big meeting" with the Smith professor.

But it's not. It's a voice mail from Kirsten, of all people. She wants to know if I've heard from Stewart.

Obviously, I have not.

I throw my phone in my backpack and roll back over.

"Whassamattah?" one of my roommates asks me, in her throaty Boston accent.

"Nothing," I say.

4

Kirsten calls me again that night. I'm in the study area in the basement of the Student Union. I go outside to take the call.

"Hey, Kirsten," I say. "What's up?"

"I'm sorry to bother you," she says. "But have you heard from Stewart by any chance?"

"No. Why?"

"He didn't come home last night."

I stand at the top of the stairs, looking down on the quad. "Did he say where he was going?" I ask.

"No. He didn't say anything."

I watch a gang of UMass students strolling by in their down vests. "Well, you know how guys are," I say.

"Have you heard from him at all?" she asks.

"No. Not since last summer."

"It's just weird, is all. I got home from work and he wasn't here, which isn't that unusual. And then I eventually went to bed, thinking he'd come in . . . you know . . . at some point."

"That's weird."

"Yeah, I get a little worried, you know. He isn't at his sister's."

"Did you try his dad?"

"I don't have his number. Do you?"

"No."

"It's probably nothing. He probably ran off somewhere. Maybe he went with those skater boys. How are things going for you? How's school?"

"Okay."

"Yeah. We've been doing pretty good. I thought we were anyway. Do you think Stewart . . . ? Do you think he would just . . . leave?"

"I don't know, Kirsten," I say. "Anything's possible."

"I mean, I know our place is small and everything. . . ."

"I have no idea. I'm three thousand miles away."

"Yeah, okay. Sorry to bother you."

"That's all right."

5

Despite a not-so-great first month, UMass begins to grow on me. A film course that seemed lame at first starts to get fun when we watch *Shampoo*. I make friends with two girls from there and we hang out a little.

I also find an AA meeting where I meet a woman named Gina, who's an Environmental Studies grad student. She's goofy and fun and we end up driving into Boston a couple times and going to see this bluegrass band she knows. She becomes my new best friend, I guess. We spend hours together, driving around, going to AA meetings, complaining about men and school and whatever else we can think of.

Then, when the semester ends, Gina invites me to come stay with her in Northampton for a week before I go home for vacation. I sleep on her couch and have a great time. We both work for a couple days at Village Books, unpacking Christmas stock. I love the bookstore and the people there, and at one point the manager asks if I would want to work there part-time next semester. This makes me feel much better about things.

Maybe I don't have to be a glamorous Smithie. Maybe I can just be my own person, living a bookstore life back east. That might be okay, I think.

6

fly home for Christmas. My parents pick me up at the airport. They're thrilled to see me. They study me, poke me, question me. I can see the wonder in their eyes. *Look at her, she's changed!* It must be weird to be a parent.

The first couple days home, I don't return any phone messages. There's a lot of them too, messages from Martin and Emily and Tara Peterson and Kirsten and even one from Simon, who goes to Reed now. But I need a little decompression time. I just want to sleep and take baths and be with my parents.

But once Christmas is over, I call people back. I don't call Kirsten, though. Or Stewart. Something is obviously up with them. Maybe they broke up. It's not really any of my business.

Instead, I hang out with other returned college students. I hang out with Martin. He's liking Stanford but he's a little shell-shocked. He's not the only genius in his world anymore.

We go to a party at Tara Peterson's. She's her usual annoying self. Grace shows up and acts like she's the most important person at the party. Other people from Evergreen show up. It's weird how people have altered themselves to fit into their different colleges. . . .

I call Simon and we have coffee. This is by far my most interesting social engagement. I tell him about UMass and my disastrous meeting with Professor Slotnik. He laughs at my story. "Think of it as initiation," he says. "They can't just let you into the club. They've got to humiliate you first."

"But she was totally superior to me! In every way."

"Those people who look so together. They're as insecure as anyone. Maybe more so. You're as smart as any of them."

"No way am I as smart as her."

"You totally are. Just wait. You'll see."

This makes me feel a little better. It makes me want to get back to school.

It also makes me like Simon. Not just for flattering me. But in general. He's just cool. And he's so easy to talk to.

I think I have a crush on him.

I n January, I return to UMass and start my second semester. I'm a little smarter about classes this term, and manage to get into a good Russian Lit course.

As the semester proceeds, I get a second chance to hang out with Smith people, since one of Gina's friends is an associate professor there and we end up at several Smith cocktail parties.

Best of all, I also take a highly recommended comparative religion class at Mount Holyoke, which is the exact scenario I wanted so badly: a small class of prissy, smart girls in pink sweaters, all worshipping at the feet of a pompous professor blathering on about himself. Why did I think this would make me happy? I do not know. It is sort of funny, though. And it gives me something to joke with Gina about.

When summer comes, Gina insists I come live with her and some other grad student friends in an old house in Northampton. I ask my parents and they are of course skeptical and worried, but I remind them: I am now nineteen. I have not been in trouble for three years. I don't drink. I get good grades. I am basically a reasonable, responsible person.

They finally agree to it, and when school lets out, I move in with Gina. This turns out to be a fantastic summer. I work part-time at Village Books and spend the other time hanging out with Gina, going to parties and concerts and drinking iced teas in the humid summer nights.

My parents still want to see me, so I go home for a week at the end of August. No one's around, though, so I don't really see anyone. I call Simon and we go on a long hike one day. Otherwise I lay low.

part nine

And so it is that an entire year passes in which I do not see or hear from Stewart or Kirsten. I do think about the call from Kirsten sometimes. They must have broken up. Poor Kirsten. Poor anyone who fell too far in love with Stewart.

Not that my own boy situation is going any better. The first semester of my sophomore year becomes my "Time of the Bad Date." It begins with three different guys asking me out in the first week of school. Michael, a senior who is very cute, turns out to be bland and smothering. Another guy, a fellow sophomore, is the guitarist in a band that turns out to be terrible and embarrassing. A third guy, who I meet at Village Books, is a cute computer guy. None of these work out, but I make out with the computer guy once, which reminds me how nice physical affection can be.

No sooner have I worked through these first three guys than new guys appear to take their place. It's a little weird. I've never been popular before. Or whatever you call it when guys show up wherever you are, with that starry look in their eyes. But that's what happens now. Maybe they were always there, and I didn't notice. Or maybe I'm just not so toxic anymore. Maybe I've healed in some way I'm not aware of.

There's one boy who I never mind hearing from: Simon. He starts e-mailing me from Reed during fall term and we end up talking on the phone on a semi-regular basis. A real friendship develops, and he's the first person I call when I go home to my parents for my sophomore winter break.

I meet him at Nordstrom for a coffee a couple days before Christmas. We sit in the upstairs café with the rich ladies and chatter happily about our college lives. He tells me about a big New Year's party his friends are having. He wants me to come.

"You remember I don't really drink, don't you?" I say.

"That's okay. I barely drink myself. Especially on New Year's. I hate champagne."

I smile when he says that. I like Simon so much. He always says the right thing. Could he become my first college boy-friend? Gina always tells me: "You're gonna have to like somebody someday."

Outside Nordstrom, we stand together on the sidewalk. It's cold, with a few tiny wisps of snow in the air. There are Christmas wreaths hanging from the streetlights above us.

I put on my hat. Simon puts on his gloves. This is when I see a little gang of street kids standing across the street at Pioneer Square. One of them is Jeff Weed. I think it is. I can't really tell. Another one also looks familiar. He's tall, lanky, I can't see his face but his stance, it reminds me of something. . . .

"It'll be a great party," Simon is saying. "And I really want you to meet my friends. You're gonna love Josh and those guys."

"It does sound like fun," I say, distracted, watching the person across the street.

"So what do you think? Wanna go?"

I'm about to answer, but at that moment, the tall, lanky guy turns in our direction. That's when I see who it is. The recognition hits me so hard it knocks the air out of my chest.

It's Stewart.

For a moment our eyes lock across the street. We're both so shocked and surprised we cannot look away. For one impossible moment, my heart leaps. I want to run to him, throw my arms around him.

But then I see him as he is: Neon blue hair. Filthy trench coat. Hollow, gaunt face.

A bottle of cheap whiskey is hanging out of his pocket.

I'm embarrassed. I'm horrified. I don't know what to do, where to look. I turn away. My heart feels like it's stopped in my chest.

"Maddie?" says Simon. "What is it?"

I have to leave. I turn and begin walking in the opposite direction. I hurry down the sidewalk, then dash through the intersection, against the light. A car slams on its brakes, honks.

Simon dodges traffic to chase me. He looks around, trying to understand what just happened.

"Maddie?" he yells. "Maddie! Wait!"

Across the street, I walk as fast as I can. I don't look back, I won't even turn my head. "I have to go," I yell to Simon as he runs to catch up. "I forgot I have to do something."

"What happened?" he asks. "What's the matter?"

I walk. My eyes fill with tears. I round a corner and I can see my car. I clear my eyes with my coat sleeves.

"Maddie . . . ?" says Simon, finally catching up.

"It's nothing," I say. "I'm fine. I'm sorry."

We get to my mom's Volvo. "No, it's okay," he says, out of breath. "You just scared me."

"I have to go," I tell him. I unlock my door. I wipe my eyes again.

"Seriously, Maddie, what is it? What just happened?"

"I'm fine. I'll call you about the party." I get in my car.

He stares. I shut the door and lower my window.

"I'm sorry," I tell him. "I get stressed out sometimes over the holidays."

He stands, baffled. But he accepts what I'm telling him.

I start the car and he moves a few steps back. "Will you call me?" he says.

I nod that I will and watch him walk away. I pretend I'm going to drive away but I don't.

When he's gone, I turn the car off. I lean my forehead against the steering wheel. I close my eyes and breathe and try to comprehend what I just saw.

2

drive home and spend the rest of the night in a daze, staring at the TV as my parents fuss around.

I tell them nothing. I don't dare.

I take a hot bath that night, brush my teeth in my brightly lit bathroom, crawl into my clean bed of fresh linen.

Outside it is cold and raining. Stewart is out there somewhere sleeping on concrete.

I toss and turn in my bed. I get up at 2:00 a.m. and call Susan, my old AA sponsor.

She is asleep but she wakes up immediately when she hears my voice.

She stays up and talks to me for an hour. She understands my situation. But she is very afraid of it.

"I know," I tell her. "But I have to go down there. I have to try to find him."

She reminds me of the drowning-man scenario. You try to save the drowning man but he grabs you, clings to you, takes you down with him.

And then you have two drowning people to contend with.

3

don't care. I'm going.

The next day, I dress for the weather: jeans, a thick sweater, my rain parka. I drive downtown.

What will I say to him? I have no idea. Why didn't I call Kirsten back a year ago? Why didn't I stay on top of that?

I park and walk the streets around Pioneer Square. That's where the street kids usually are. They are here today too, little pockets of them, like litters of abandoned puppies.

I walk through the square. I walk farther downtown. I find the shop where Kirsten sold flowers. A girl is helping customers. I approach her. "Do you know a girl named Kirsten? That used to work here?"

"No, but the woman back there probably does."

I go to the back of the shop. There's an older woman there, moving bags of dirt around.

"Do you know Kirsten?"

The woman looks back at me. "Yes. What about her?"

"Does she still work here?"

"No. Not anymore."

"Do you know where she is?"

"I would guess she went home to Centralia." The woman avoids looking at me. She looks sad, though. She must have liked Kirsten.

Kirsten was a sweet girl. *I hope she's okay, wherever she is,* I think to myself.

An hour later I find Stewart.

He's on the River Walk with four other guys under the Morrison Bridge. They're sitting on the cement wall, out of the rain. One of them has a skateboard; they're taking turns on it. They drink beer from forties they have stashed in brown paper bags.

I walk up slowly, my hands in my pockets, my clean, college-girl hair neatly tucked under my clean, college-girl hat.

Stewart wears fingerless gloves, the same ragged trench coat, a black hoodie underneath. He doesn't see me at first. He takes the skateboard from a short Mexican and rides it in circles, doing kick turns and nearly falling off backward.

I walk closer and then stop, standing on the edge of this gang, watching them. They are hardened streeters. They are some scary dudes.

The short Mexican is the first to notice me. "Hey, señorita!" he calls to me.

I say nothing. The other guys gawk at me. Finally, Stewart turns. When he sees me the others grow quiet.

Without taking his eyes off me, he reaches for his forty, takes a deep swig of it, and replaces it on the wall.

He belches loudly.

"That ain't no way to address a fine chica like that!" jokes the Mexican kid.

Stewart says nothing. He stares at me. He's still tall. He's still imposing. But now he looks like a skeleton.

He begins to walk toward me. My heart skips a beat. The bottoms of my feet tingle with fear.

But I stand my ground.

"What do you want?" he says.

"Nothing," I answer. "I . . . wanted to see you."

"What for?"

"No reason."

He looks over my head for a moment, like he doesn't know if it's worth wasting five minutes talking to me.

"You got a cigarette?" he says.

"I don't smoke. Remember?"

He leads me away from his friends. We walk across the grass toward Front Avenue. He stops at a little store to get cigarettes, but he only has a dollar, so I put in four dollars of my own.

He takes the pack and we walk to another little park, also covered. He seems to know all the places where there's shelter from the rain. We sit on a bench and he lights a cigarette with dirty, knobby fingers.

"I saw you last night with your boyfriend," he says.

"He's not my boyfriend."

He smokes. Slowly I begin to look at him. He's deeply dirty, the way homeless people are. His face, so young and carefree before, now looks ravaged. His eyes shine in a sickening way, as if they want to burn themselves out as fast as humanly possible.

It's too much. I can't face him. I look away.

"What's the matter with you?" he asks.

I shrug. "You don't look too good," I say into the ground.

"Yeah? Well, life's not too good at the moment."

"You look like a junkie."

"Well, I am a junkie. What did you think I was?"

I say nothing.

He smokes.

We sit and watch the rain falling in the street.

"You look different too," Stewart says when we're walking again. "You look older."

"I am older."

The rain has let up for a moment. We walk in the open air. You can see patches of fog in the hills above the city.

"How's college?" he asks.

"Good."

"You learnin' anything?"

"Probably not. But it's good. It's a good life."

He's so skinny, so starved. I want to buy him some food. I delicately steer us toward a burrito trailer I saw earlier. Without asking him, I stop and casually order us two burritos.

"What happened to Kirsten?" I ask.

"She left."

"She called me. Like a year ago."

"Yeah, that's what she said. She said you didn't want to talk to her. She said you didn't care about us anymore. You'd washed your hands of us."

"That's not true," I say.

"That's what she said."

"Don't be like that. I did my best with her. You know that."

"She sure thought the world of you. She couldn't shut up about you going back east to college. I tried to tell her the truth. You were born into that. Your dad's a rich business guy."

I say nothing. I take our two burritos and lead him to a covered table where I'm hoping he'll eat.

"What are you gonna do now?" I ask, pushing his burrito toward him.

He ignores the food. He lights another cigarette.

"You can't stay on the street forever," I say.

"You're right about that. People die down here. That Mexican kid I was with just now? A cop tried to run him down last week, tried to kill him with his car. Fuckin' pigs. We have ways, though. We're not as helpless as we seem. We can make you pay, if you mess with us."

I watch his face as he says this. I've never heard him talk like this before. He's like a totally different person.

I set down my burrito. "Stewart?"

"Yeah?"

I choose my words carefully. I speak as clearly and calmly as I can. "Whatever you think you see right now. This whole situation. Whatever you think is right or logical or makes sense . . . none of it is real. It's an illusion. You can walk right out of here. You can go back to Spring Meadow. You can clean up. You've done it before. You know that it works."

"I can't, though," he says.

"Why can't you?"

"Because. It's just delaying things. It's delaying the inevitable. This is where I'm supposed to be."

"But it's not, though. You know that. I know that. We forget. Of course we do. I forgot that time I got drunk at that party. You forgot that time in Redland. That's why we have to stick together."

He stares into the distance.

"You don't have to do this," I say. "My car is four blocks from here. We can just walk up the street, get in my car, and drive to a detox. And then this whole nightmare is over. We can end it right now. In the next twenty minutes."

He shakes his head. "I . . . I can't. . . ."

"Why can't you?"

"Well, look at me. You have eyes!"

I absorb this sudden outburst. I remain calm, patient, clear. "You're right, you look terrible. But it doesn't matter. Not in the slightest."

He thinks about this. He knows I'm right. I can see that it's sinking in.

But then he takes a violent hit off his cigarette. "I cheated on you. You know that, don't you?"

"Stewart, it doesn't matter. None of that matters."

"But it does matter. Because I screwed you over! And then I screwed Kirsten over!"

"Nobody cares."

"Kirsten cares. Just ask her if she cares. You don't know what I did to her. I stole from her. I took her rent money that she made selling flowers. I lied to her face."

"Those things are fixable. The point is, nobody wants you to die out here. Not her. Not me. Not the people in Centralia. Remember those people? At the AA meeting? How proud they were of you? People care about you, Stewart. People *love* you. Don't you know that?"

Suddenly his face changes. He's pissed. He stands up, throws down his cigarette, and begins striding back toward the river.

I jump up too. I hurry after him.

"Kirsten made you do this," he snarls at me.

"No," I plead. "It's not true!"

"You're both just trying to get back at me. I'm not going to be some pawn in your game. You can't control me."

He suddenly turns back toward me. He looks like a man possessed. His face has become an ugly, twisted sneer. That phrase people use: *He was struggling with his demons.* I see them. I can see the actual demons.

"Come down here on your high horse," he growls. "Telling me what I have to do. What about you? What do you have to do? Huh? Why don't you take some responsibility for what goes on around here? The cops almost killed my friend. They think they own the streets. They don't own nothing!"

I stand there, staring at this person, this crazy street person.

For a brief moment, I don't see anyone I recognize.

He won't come with me. He walks back toward the river and I follow him, though he isn't speaking anymore. I try to give him money but he slaps the bills out of my hand. He tells me to get away from him. He never wants to see me again. He hates me. He spits on the ground at my feet.

I stop then. I let him go. . . .

5

The next day, I try again. I park and walk around Pioneer Square. I check the River Walk. I see other street kids, other homeless people, but I can't find Stewart.

I try the skate park across the river. I see Jeff Weed in the afternoon and ask him.

"Yeah, he's been around," says Jeff, unsure of what my purpose is. "Don't know where he is today."

For the most part, people try to help. One kid says he may have left town. I can't tell if this is true or if he's been told to say it.

I finally give up and go into a Starbucks downtown. I get coffee and sit at the window and call Susan. Then I call Gina in Northampton.

"You gotta prepare yourself, Maddie," Gina tells me.

"For what?"

"You know."

This sends me into a panic. "He's not going to die down here! I won't let him!"

"He's going to do what he's going to do. And you can't stop him."

Later, in my car, I see the short Mexican kid from under the bridge. I honk and pull over and try to talk to him, but he runs away when he sees me.

I run after him. I chase him down the street. "No, I'm your friend!" I yell. "I'm the chica from yesterday!"

He vanishes down an alley.

That night, I track down Kirsten on the computer and call her at her mom's house in Centralia. She's pregnant by a new boyfriend. She hasn't talked to Stewart in a year. She thinks he got into drugs again. In any event, he stopped living in their apartment and paying their bills. She was forced to move home.

"I miss him, though," she tells me in a shaky voice. "Have you seen him?"

"Just once."

"Is he bad?"

"Yeah. Pretty bad," I tell her.

"Thanks for trying to help him. I would come down there, but my mom doesn't think I should. You know, with the baby coming."

"Yeah," I tell her.

I spend a couple more days wandering around downtown. But time is running out. He's obviously left the area, or made it impossible for me to find him. And I have to go back to my own life. Both Susan and Gina are adamant about that. *I have to go back to UMass.*

On the last day of my vacation, I set my suitcase on my bed and begin organizing my stuff. As I do, a rush of panic comes over me. I can't leave him here. I *can't*.

But even as I think this, even as tears form in my eyes and fall into my suitcase, my hands continue to pack.

6

I fly back east, over the clouds, a perfect blue sky enveloping me, cleansing me, freeing me from my past.

At least that's what it feels like.

Gina picks me up at the airport. There is nothing to say. She knows how hard it is. We exchange a long and tearful hug.

It's good to be home. Our off-campus house is my home now. More than my parents' house. It's where I feel the most like myself. I lie in my bed here, surrounded by my books, my plants, my laptop. I have become a new person in my time at UMass. I was right to come here.

After a couple days, I get back into school stuff. I pick my new classes. I find out I've been admitted to an advanced Emily Dickinson class at Amherst College. So that's good news.

The day before the semester begins, Gina takes me out to dinner. We talk about normal things: a guy she met over vacation, a new professor in her department.

She thinks I should date this semester. She thinks some new romantic possibilities would be good for my mental health.

I don't know how that's going to work. I couldn't even make it to Simon's New Year's party. She's probably right, though. I resolve to get a haircut, and buy some new sneakers.

Sure enough, I get asked out twice in the first week of school. I say yes in both cases, and politely sit with both of the young men, drinking coffee and smiling at the appropriate times.

But I still think about Stewart. I think about him every day. The New England sky is so different from the Pacific Northwest. It makes him seem so far away.

Then one Tuesday night after dinner, I find myself walking across campus to the far edge of town. I do this because I saw an old movie theater there and I want to check it out.

It's a long walk, but I'm happy for the exercise. I feel strangely at peace. I'm not lonely tonight. I'm going to the movies.

The theater is called The Academy. It's a lot like The Carlton. I pay my five bucks and get some cheap popcorn. I thank the local girl who stuffs my bag until it's overflowing.

Inside the theater, I sit by myself near the back, a dozen other people scattered around me. The lights go down and I begin chomping popcorn and letting my brain drift slowly into the story.

The next Tuesday, I do it again. I walk across campus, through the cold, to The Academy theater. It's a good way to relax, get away from campus, take a break from the pressures of college life.

It's something I still do to this day. Not every Tuesday, but a lot of them. Movie night. And of course I think of Stewart whenever I go. Maybe I'm waiting for him to come join me, come sit with me, come flop his big feet over the seats in front.

That's the thing: You can change things. You can repair mistakes. You can restart your whole life if you have to.

But some things you never get back. Certain people. Certain moments in time when you don't know better than to shield your heart.

You don't see those moments coming, you don't know it when they're happening, but later, as the plainness of life begins to show itself, you realize how important they were. You understand who really changed you, who made you what you are.

And so I never really say good-bye to Stewart. I keep him inside me. My first love. My best friend. My Lost Prince.

And if he ever returns he'll know where to find me. The Academy theater. I'm still here. Feet up. Chomping stale popcorn. Saving him a seat.

BLAKE NELSON is the author of many acclaimed novels, including *Destroy All Cars*, *Girl*, *Rock Star Superstar*, *Paranoid Park,* and *The Prince of Venice Beach*. He lives in Portland, Oregon, but you can visit him on the web at www.blakenelsonbooks.com.